KISSED
— by —
ICE

SUNWALKER SAGA - BOOK FIVE

SHÉA MACLEOD

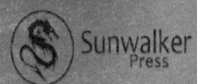

Sunwalker
Press

Kissed by Ice
Sunwalker Saga Book Five
Text copyright © 2014 Shéa MacLeod
All rights reserved.
Printed in the United States of America.

Cover Art by Amanda Kelsey of Razzle Dazzle Designs
Editing by Theo Fenraven
Proof reading by Jenx Byron
Formatted by PyperPress

DEDICATION

This book is dedicated to those who give their lives every day to protect us from the monsters. Thank you just doesn't seem like enough.

ACKNOWLEDGMENTS

A big THANK YOU to Bonne, Ed, and Xtine who read one form of this story or another and gave me their honest (and sometimes brutal) feedback. If it wasn't for you, this book wouldn't be half as good.

A thanks to my super awesome cover artist, editor, and proof reader who put their hearts and souls into their work. You guys are awesome!

And, of course, a super big thank you to my family and friends, who put up with my foibles and fripperies on a semi-daily basis. Without your love and support, I'd have never gotten this far.

Shéa MacLeod

Previously...

I'd just stepped out of the shower in my Paris hotel room when my laptop chimed. Someone was trying to Skype me. I quickly threw on my robe and wrapped my hair in a towel before answering the call.

"Eddie!" I smiled as his face appeared on my screen. The connection was a little iffy, the picture and sound freezing and jumping around. "How are you? Aren't you on that steampunk cruise in the Caribbean?" Eddie Mulligan, my friend and the owner of a new age shop in Portland, was a steampunk enthusiast. I hadn't expected to hear from him while he was on his cruise.

"Yes, in the Bahamas. Morgan, listen carefully. I..." The image froze for a second. "... danger. Discovered..." It froze again, this time for longer. I uselessly thumped the side of my screen as if it might help.

"Eddie? Are you there?"

"Need...help. Come quickly...dead."

"What? Eddie? Oh my gods, what's happening?"

There was a bit more jumping around of the screen, and then it zoomed in on one of Eddie's bespectacled eyes. "Hurry, Morgan. If you don't, we're all dead."

With that, the connection dropped entirely. No matter what I tried, I couldn't get him back.

I stared at the blank screen before giving myself a mental kick in the pants. I had to get to the Bahamas as fast as I could. I started running around the room, grabbing my things and throwing them randomly in my suitcase.

Airport. I needed to get to the airport. I could use the private plane Jack and I had taken to France. What island? I

1

needed to find out where the ship was and fly to the nearest island. But what cruise line had Eddie taken?

Jack. I needed Jack.

I dashed out my door and down the hall to pound on his door. "Jack. Jack! Are you in there?" There was no answer. "Dammit."

I ran back to my room and grabbed my phone. I noticed I had a voicemail, but I didn't take the time to listen. I needed to find out where Eddie was. Before I could dial, it rang. I frowned, not recognizing the number. I did recognize the country code, though. It was someone in the UK.

"Hello?"

"Morgan? This is Drago."

"Drago, hi. Listen..."

"I need you to come to Scotland as quickly as possible."

"I can't." I tossed a boot into my suitcase, then pulled it back out when I realized I'd need to wear it. "I have to catch a flight..."

"Yes, you do. To Edinburgh as fast as you can." I heard the urgency in his voice, and my blood ran cold.

"What's wrong, Drago?"

"It's Inigo."

CHAPTER ONE

"What is it? What's wrong with Inigo?" I gripped the phone so tightly I could hear the plastic cracking in protest.

"Just come, Morgan. Quickly."

"What's wrong with Inigo?" I practically yelled into the phone. Drago didn't hear me. He'd already hung up, leaving me about five seconds from a full-blown panic attack.

Screaming just about every cuss word I knew, I continued throwing random items in my suitcase. I knew I was freaking out, but I didn't know what to do about it. Eddie was somewhere in the Bahamas dying or something. The love of my life was lying in a death coma in the Highlands of Scotland from which he may or may not ever emerge. I needed to be in two places at once, and my so-called Sunwalker guardian, Jack, was nowhere to be found. I let out another shriek of frustration as I slammed my bag closed and zipped it shut. What the hell was I going to do?

Deep breath, Morgan. Deep breath. I forced myself to think somewhat logically. Kabita, my best friend and boss at the so-called private investigation firm where we both worked (it was in reality a front for our true activities: hunting vampires, demons, and other things that went bump in the night.), was still back in Portland, and she was a hell of a lot closer to the Bahamas than I was, so I dialed her number.

"Do you know what time this is?" She sounded like death warmed over. Kabita was no more a morning person than I was. According to my calculations, it was about four a.m. back in Portland.

3

"You need to get to the Bahamas."

A moment of silence. "Good morning to you, too, Morgan."

"Eddie's on that damned steampunk cruise, and he called me. Something about people dying. He needed me to come urgently."

"So I need to come why?"

"Because," I said as I grabbed my bag and headed downstairs to get a taxi, "I have to go to Scotland."

Another beat of silence. "Inigo."

"Yes."

"Is he...?"

"I don't know," I admitted. "All Drago would say was to come. He hung up before I could get anything else out of him." And for that I was seriously going to read him the riot act. I mentally sent the dragon king a few choice mental curses.

"What about Jack? Can't he go?"

"I can't find him. He disappeared a few hours ago and he's not answering his phone. Besides, you're closer. I have a feeling this thing with Eddie is time sensitive." Understatement of the year.

There was a beat of silence. "I'm on my way."

"I don't know what cruise line he's on."

"I'll figure it out."

I knew I could count on her. Outside the hotel I hailed a cab and spent the entire cab ride on the phone with the airline. An insane amount of money later, I was in possession of an e-ticket for a flight to Edinburgh. An hour later I was through security and found myself strapped into the world's tiniest seat on the world's smallest airplane.

4

I closed my eyes as another air pocket sent the tiny plane-let plummeting toward the earth before it bounced back into place. The arm rests dug into my hips and my lower back already hurt from the odd curvature of the seat backs. I muttered a few choice words under my breath. If I ever got my hands on Jackson Keel again, I was going to kill him. Granted, he'd just come back to life—the immortal bastard—but it would still hurt like hell. He deserved it, the big jerk. Making me fly commercial. When I got my hands on him....

I shifted uneasily in the narrow seat. There was so little padding, it was only marginally better than sitting on a cheap metal folding chair. My butt was going numb. Scratch that. My butt had gone numb thirty minutes ago, and it was starting to ache where I'd busted my coccyx during a Hunt over a year ago. Damn vampire had jumped out of nowhere and sent me flying flat on my ass.

If Jack hadn't vanished from our Paris hotel, I'd be on a private plane right now. One with cushy seats and no need to explain my suitcase full of weapons. As it was, I'd had to leave everything behind at the hotel, along with a hefty tip so they wouldn't do something like call the police or try to sell my knives on eBay. Thanks to Jack I was not only freaked out, but weaponless, devoid of cash, and airsick.

I fidgeted with my cell phone, anxious to email Kabita. I wanted to check if she'd landed in Miami yet even though I knew she was still in midair. There was no point in calling. And besides, the plane-let didn't have that nifty mid-air Wi-Fi the big planes had these days. Stupid cheap-ass airline.

I tried to entertain myself with all the ways I was going to throttle Jack when I found him, but all I could focus on was the Skype call from Eddie, followed by the phone call from Drago. Had I made the right choice?

The tiny aircraft hit another air pocket, sending my stomach soaring into my throat. I swallowed back the bile and started calculating the various ways to kill a vampire. Anything to distract myself from the thought of heaving up my last meal. Hey, whatever works, right?

The minute the plane touched down in Edinburgh, I was out of my seat and collecting my bags. Fortunately I hadn't brought anything that needed to be checked. Customs was slow, but pretty much a breeze, and soon I was headed through the terminal toward the taxi stand.

"Morgan? Morgan Bailey?"

I turned toward the voice, surprised to hear someone call my name. He was tall. Probably six foot four or so, and built like those big-ass guys who throw trees around at the Highland Games. His hair was red, and his skin was that warm golden brown studded with freckles that some redheads are lucky enough to have. His eyes, like mine, were green, but where mine were kind of a cool ocean green with a bit of gray, his were the warmer mossy green of the forest.

He held out one very large hand. "Finn Campbell," he said, giving my hand a good, hearty shake. I caught a whiff of campfires and vanilla. "Drago sent me."

Of course. He was dragon kin, but not related to Drago and Inigo. Men of their line had a hint of chocolate to their natural scent. "Hi. Nice to meet you."

He took my bag and ushered me toward a black Mercedes with an almost courtly air. It was very old school, but it was likely Finn himself was old school. After all, dragons lived for centuries. He may not look a day over thirty, but he could have been around when the first European settlers set foot in the Americas.

"What's going on with Inigo?" I asked once we were inside his car. "Is he all right?"

Finn gave me an apologetic look. "I'm sorry. There is nothing I can say."

That was a weird way to phrase it. "Nothing you *can* say? Or nothing you *will* say?"

"I've got my orders."

I quite possibly said something rude. He ignored me.

"You might as well get comfortable," Finn said, unperturbed. "We've got a four-hour drive ahead of us."

"Can't you just fly?" I asked. "It would be a hell of a lot faster." I'd flown with Inigo before when he was in dragon form. It was a little on the chilly side, but crazy fast.

Finn shot me a sideways look. "Can you imagine the reaction if the locals saw a dragon flying around in broad daylight?" His heavy burr was tinged with amusement.

"Okay, good point," I admitted with a sigh.

"Why don't you try and get some sleep?" Finn suggested.

It was my turn to give him a sideways look. Was he serious? My mind was a whirlwind of worry and fear over both Inigo and Eddie, and Finn expected me to *sleep*? What did he know that I didn't? My stomach started churning again. Gods, I could use an antacid. Scratch that. An entire bottle of them.

The drive was an exercise in both self-control and mental torture. Self-control in that I didn't puke all over everything—hurray for motion sickness—and mental

7

torture in that I couldn't stop thinking of all the possible things that could be so very wrong that Drago would need me to drop everything and rush to Scotland. But finally, as the car rounded a final bend, the castle that was the dragon kin stronghold came into view. The car slid beneath the ancient portcullis and came to a stop in a cobbled courtyard. The stone keep soared above us in a display of looming intimidation, the dark stone gloomy against the overcast sky. A few pots of what looked like they'd once been pansies lined the sweeping staircase that led to the front door. Unfortunately, it looked like someone had taken a blow torch to them. I supposed that was the danger to any plant life in a fortress full of dragons.

"You go ahead," Finn said. "I'll make sure your bag gets to your room."

With a nod of thanks, I swung open the car door and stepped out into the cool Highland air.

# # #

"Morgan." Drago stood at the top of the front steps of the castle, bracketed on either side by a pair of massive carved stone dragons. He was in human form, but his eyes glittered an eerie gold as they caught sunlight. His dragon was close to the surface. But then, it always was. That was why he was king.

"Drago, what the hell is going on?" I demanded as I jogged up the steps to join him. Despite barely coming to his shoulder, I propped my hands on my hips and glared at him.

His smile was a little tight. "I think you should see for yourself." He turned and strode into the castle keep, clearly expecting me to follow.

I assumed he would take me to the caves where the dragons kept their healing eggs. I remembered very clearly the last time I'd been there. Inigo had been inside one of those eggs for the last few months, healing from having his heart practically ripped out of his chest. Instead Drago lead me down a long hall deeper inside the castle. Other than the occasional electric sconces, the hall was nearly dark. On either side of the hall hung portraits of what I could only assume were previous dragon kings or council elders. They were exquisitely painted in bright colors, each housed in a rich, gilt frame. I stopped to peer at one and realized it wasn't gilt at all, but pure gold. Maybe the legends about dragons and their hordes weren't that far off.

Overhead the ceiling soared in a series of high arches that would have done a gothic cathedral proud. Hanging from each beam was an elegant chandelier dripping with crystals. I wondered vaguely if they were real crystals or if they were actually diamonds. I wouldn't put it past the drags. The floor was of simple stone but covered over in thick, lush Persian carpets. From what I could tell in the dim light, they were old and handmade. Probably worth a fortune, like the gold frames and the chandeliers.

It felt like we walked for ages before Drago took an abrupt right onto a wide flight of stairs leading upward. The stone steps had been left bare, and I saw slight depressions in the center where generations of feet had tread the same path over and over, wearing down the stone. The electric sconces continued up the stairs, but these had been turned off. Instead, tiny rays of sunlight trickled through extremely narrow windows high in the stone walls. I remembered those windows from other castles I'd visited on my historically inspired rambles back when I had time for such things. They were arrow slits.

At the top of the stairs was another wide hall. The walls were lined with elegantly carved wooden doors. The floor was stone, covered with thick rugs like below, but the stone walls had been plastered over and painted with brightly colored murals. Here there was a thicket of trees, a dragon's tail sticking out from between the trunks; there a patch of bright blue sky with half a dozen dragons in flight, each of them a different color, scales shining in the light of the painted sun. The artwork was beyond breathtaking to the point of being magical. The dragons felt almost alive. My fingers itched to reach out and touch their shimmering scales.

I wondered what the hell was going on. Why had Drago brought me here? Where was Inigo?

Halfway down the hall, Drago stopped and rapped gently on one of the doors. It swung open to reveal a woman dressed in purple scrubs, her gray-streaked hair scooped up in a bun. On a black cord around her neck hung a gold medallion with a symbol in blue enamel: the Eye of Horus. A symbol used by healers and mystics since the days of ancient Eygpt.

"My lord." She gave Drago a slight bow.

"How is my brother?"

"Quiet. More at ease than since he first woke."

"Inigo's awake?" I moved forward, trying to push past Drago and the woman, but he held me back.

"Morgan, this is Dalinda. She is one of our healers."

Dalinda shot Drago a look before reaching out to shake my hand. "Among normal people I'd be called a doctor, but you know how dragons love their traditions."

"Doctor?" I asked. "Why does Inigo need a doctor? What is going on? Is he okay?"

Drago and Dalinda exchanged another look. "Like I said, you should see for yourself." Drago waved toward the open door.

With a glance at the two of them, I stepped inside. The room was even darker than the hall. Heavy drapes had been pulled over the large window opposite the door, and the room was nearly overcrowded by an enormous four-poster bed. I moved closer to the bed, straining, despite my superior night vision, to make out the figure huddled under the blankets.

"Drago?" A pale face turned toward me.

"Oh my gods, Inigo." He was so much thinner than I remembered. Almost fragile-looking. But he was alive. Oh, dear gods, he was alive.

With a squeal of joy, I jumped on the bed and wrapped my arms around him, peppering his face with kisses. It took me a while to realize he wasn't kissing me back. In fact, his whole body was rigid.

"Inigo?" I backed away but kept my hands on his shoulders, reluctant to let him go entirely. "What's wrong?" I asked.

"Nothing. I'm fine." But his voice was stiff.

I withdrew my hands from his shoulders, feeling suddenly awkward. "You're acting like I'm a stranger. Don't you know who I am?"

"Of course. Morgan." But the words were cool and indifferent. "Thank you for coming, but I'm tired. I'd like to sleep now." And with that he rolled over and turned his back to me, leaving me staring at him in the dark.

Chapter Two

My cell phone rang as I stepped out into the hallway. I didn't want to take it, but my screen told me it was Kabita. With a quick glance in my direction, Dalinda bustled back into Inigo's room. Maybe she was worried I was going to have a mental breakdown or something. Drago touched my arm lightly before joining her, shutting the door to give me some privacy.

"Hi, Kabita."

"What's wrong?"

Crap. I might have known she'd hear it in my voice. There wasn't much I could get past her. "Nothing. I'm just tired, that's all. Been a long day."

"How's Inigo?"

"He's awake."

"Oh, thank goddess."

I smiled a little. "I know, right?"

"Why are you talking to me, then? Why aren't you with him?"

"He's sleeping," I lied. "I guess that egg thing takes a lot out of you. But he's fine, and that's what matters." It was all that mattered. For now. The rest would come later. I had to believe that. "Are you in Miami?"

"Just landed. Plane leaves for Nassau in a little over an hour. From there I should be able to find out where the ship is and take a helicopter out. I'll call as soon as I find Eddie and figure out what the hell is going on."

"Okay, good. I'm, uh, I should go. Just in case he wakes up."

13

"Tell him 'hi' from me."

"Will do." Once I figured out what the bloody hell was going on.

Kabita hung up, and I shoved my phone back in my jeans pocket. I dithered in the hallway a minute, not sure what to do. Clearly Inigo didn't want me in his room, but I wanted to know what was going on. I was his girlfriend, after all. I loved him, and he loved me. Or he had before everything had gone to hell in a hand basket, and he'd ended up mostly dead, bleeding out on the high desert.

I was going in, dammit. I started toward the door, but it swung open before I could get to it. Drago stepped out, closing the door behind him. He gave me a long look.

"Come, Morgan. We need to talk."

# # #

"What the hell is going on, Drago?"

We were ensconced in what could only be described as Drago's man cave. Except, of course, it was far more extravagant than any man cave I'd ever seen. Tall arched windows rose gracefully toward the high ceiling, filling the space with light. Between the half dozen windows, every square inch of wall space was covered in bookshelves crammed with leather-bound volumes, some of them quite old. The only wall that wasn't covered was a large rectangle above the massive stone fireplace where he'd hung an enormous flat screen television. The thing looked completely out of place for the old castle and yet totally in keeping with a man cave.

14

Around the fireplace was gathered a collection of plush leather couches and chairs interspersed with small tables for holding beverages and snacks. There was even one of those cool globes that was really a bar. Drago struck me as a whisky man. The other side of the room was taken over by a massive desk of some kind of dark wood, richly stained and intricately carved with depictions of—what else?—dragons. It looked like it belonged in a museum.

I lounged in one of the overstuffed chairs by the unlit fire. Drago shoved a glass of something alcoholic in my hand before taking the seat opposite. I gave it a sniff. Port. One of my favorites. Not that I felt much like drinking. Still, I took a small sip to fortify myself.

"Come on, tell me. What is going on?" I repeated.

Drago sighed and took a long swallow of his drink. I'd been right about the whisky. Finally he said, "Inigo woke yesterday a few hours before I called you. He was extremely disoriented at first. Weak. Feverish. I called in Dalinda immediately. At first we weren't sure he'd make it."

My heart gave a painful lurch. I should have been there. "Is this, ah, normal?"

"Not exactly. But like I told you when we put him in the egg, he's only half dragon. His human side made the healing unpredictable. We had no way of knowing how he would respond. In fact, if you will recall, I wasn't sure he'd wake up at all."

I nodded. He had told me, but I'd hoped for the best. It was all I had. "Obviously he made it. Physically anyway."

He gave me a long look. "Yes. Physically he is fine. Weak, perhaps, but he will regain his strength in time and with the proper therapy."

"Mentally he's not fine, is he?" I didn't really need him to answer. I'd seen for myself. But I wanted him to confirm it.

"No. He isn't."

I swallowed another bracing mouthful of port. "What's wrong with him?"

"We're not certain," Drago admitted. "Other than he seems detached from, well, just about everything and everyone. Dalinda is worried that if he does not shake loose from whatever this is, he will begin to physically decline."

"What can we do?"

He shook his head. "I do not know. And neither does Dalinda."

"Surely there is someone who does. Someone who can help. Some magic or something. What about Tanith?" Tanith was my friend Cordelia Nightwing's sister and had once gone by the name Sandra. That was how I'd first met her before she'd joined the dragons full-time as a dragon child. I'd seen her only once since then, but she'd seemed content in her role as mediator between the dragons and Britain's answer to the SRA (Supernatural Regulatory Agency), the human-run MI8. She knew things no normal human could possibly know.

"She has been unable to discern any way of helping him, unfortunately." Drago took another long swallow of his whisky, brooding eyes on the empty fireplace. "And believe me, she has tried until she has exhausted herself. I had to order her to bed and leave my mate to guard her lest she try again."

16

I'd never met Drago's wife, the dragon queen, but I'd heard stories. If they were even half right, she was one scary-ass woman. Dragon. Whatever.

"Someone has to know what to do." I repeated it like a mantra, wanting it to be true.

Drago glanced at me. "Not that I'm aware of. We've never had a situation like this. Not with a Halfling."

"Yeah, yeah," I muttered. "If he was full dragon you'd know what to do. Blah blah."

He winced a little. "It is, most unfortunately, true."

I stared at Drago. "What can I do?"

"Nothing."

I opened my mouth to argue, but Drago held up his hand.

"Time, Morgan. Give him time. Surely there is work you should be doing? At least until Inigo is ready."

He was right. Of course he was. I was a Hunter, and my job didn't go away because my boyfriend was recovering from having his heart ripped out by the Fairy Queen. "I spoke to Eddie right before you called me."

"And?"

"And right now Eddie is on a boat in the middle of the Atlantic Ocean, and something has gone extremely wrong. He may be in serious danger. Kabita's on the way, but I have no idea what kind of situation she's walking into. She shouldn't go alone."

Drago stood up. "Then we'd better get going, don't you think?"

###

"You have got to be kidding me." I eyed Drago's massive form with something surprisingly close to horror. Killing vampires was one thing. Riding dragons was another. Granted, I'd ridden Inigo in dragon form clear across the United States and the Atlantic Ocean, no less. And yes, I'd even suggested riding Finn from the airport, but Drago's dragon form made Inigo's seem downright puny. I squinted against the late afternoon sun bouncing off the dragon king's gold scales. He was the size of a small mountain. "How the hell am I supposed to get on his back? I need a freaking ladder truck."

Finn shrugged. "Easy." He grabbed me around the waist and tossed me up onto Drago's back like I was a rag doll. Unfortunately, I had no idea what I was doing. My hands slipped against smooth scales, and I slid down Drago's side like I was on one of those giant amusement park slides. I had visualized myself crashing to the ground and breaking a leg when Finn snatched me out of midair.

"When I throw you up, take hold of one of his scales," Finn snapped. "Get your fingers underneath it and use it as a handhold."

Without waiting to see if I was ready, he tossed me up again. This time I grabbed hold of one of Drago's plate-like scales, barely managing to avoid sliding off the other side and onto the cobblestone courtyard, possibly landing on my head.

I glared down at Finn. "Next time give me a warning, why don't you?" He shrugged again and ambled back inside the castle. With a sigh, I heaved myself up and onto Drago's back, using his scales to pull myself along. I seated myself just behind his shoulder ridge. Someone had threaded a tether through the scales. Once I snapped myself in, I hollered down at Drago. "Okay. Ready when you are."

If it had been Inigo, he'd have been able to mind speak, but either Drago couldn't do it with me or didn't want to. He let out a large grunt and gathered his haunches beneath him. I felt the thick muscles gather beneath my thighs, the shift and slide of scales, and then in one leap, he was in the air, wings spreading to catch the updraft off the mountainside.

Up he surged, higher and higher into the atmosphere until we were so far above the earth, the thin air turned nearly to ice. Or at least it seemed so to me. Despite my borrowed riding gear, I was turning numb from the cold. Even the thick, fur-lined gloves did little to dispel the chill. I was pretty sure my ears were going to fall off at any moment.

And then the chill was gone, replaced with a tingling warmth. The air grew thicker, easier to breath. I glanced around to see that both Drago and I were surrounded by a shimmering bubble. Inigo had thrown up one of those bubbles, too. Not only did it keep us warm and help us breathe, though Drago didn't need it nearly as much as I did, but it prevented pesky things like airplanes and radar from seeing us. The last thing we needed was the Royal Air Force freaking out about a giant dragon invading their air space. I couldn't even imagine the tabloid response to such a thing.

The other thing the bubble did was allow him to travel at full speed without turning me into a blender full of goo. The flight that should have taken something like fifteen hours by plane only took about two by dragon. My butt was just getting numb when Drago began circling, spiraling down slowly toward the sparkling blue ocean below. As we flew lower, the air grew increasingly humid and hot until I was sweating like a pig under my heavy layers of clothing.

At first I wasn't sure where Drago was headed, but then I saw the tiny little speck of white in the middle of the vast ocean between two tiny green islands. As we drew closer, the ship got bigger and bigger until I could clearly see the helo pad beneath us, rushing up fast. I opened my mouth to warn Drago, but it was too late. He landed with a thump hard enough to send me sliding off his side. Only the tether kept me from slamming into the deck. I dangled in midair for a moment before managing to unclip the tether. I fell the rest of the way to the deck, hitting hard enough to jar bone.

"Holy shit, Drago." I glanced around to see if anyone had seen us. Apparently no one had noticed a giant dragon landing on the ship as everyone was going about their business. I guess Drago still had the bubble up. I staggered to my feet, expecting to find a massive dragon on the deck. Instead he was standing there in human form, dressed in the jeans and cable knit sweater he'd been wearing at the castle.

"Damn, it's warm here," he said, pulling off the sweater to reveal a tight, black T-shirt beneath. Poor thing was stretched to the limit trying to contain his rippling chest muscles. I was kind of glad Inigo hadn't inherited his brother's size. I liked my men on the lean side.

"I thought you liked it warm," I said, shucking my flight clothes. I wished I'd had shorts or something. Boots and jeans weren't exactly meant for the tropics.

"Warm and dry. This humidity is bullshit."

Couldn't argue with him there. "We need to find Kabita, if she's here, and Eddie." I pulled out my cell phone.

He laid his hand on mine. "Won't work until I lower my shields."

What was he? A freaking starship? "Uh, okay. So lower them."

"Not here. Don't you think people would be a bit surprised to suddenly find two strangers standing in their midst?"

Frankly, I doubted it. Most people couldn't see two feet in front of their noses. "Fine." I tucked the heavy flight clothes under my arm, grabbed his hand, and pulled him into a stairwell. "Okay, this ought to be safe enough."

He nodded. There was a slight shimmer in the air. "We can be seen and heard now."

I glanced at my phone, selecting Kabita's number first. There was no answer.

"She may still be on her way," Drago pointed out. "After all, it would have taken her awhile to convince someone to give her the ship's location and then find a means of transport."

He had a point. I dialed Eddie next. Again no answer. I was starting to feel that sick queasiness in the pit of my stomach. I wasn't sure if I should chalk it up to a sudden onset of seasickness or my sixth sense telling me something was wrong. Based on past experience, I was going with the latter. Although I really wished I'd thought to bring along some Dramamine.

"Surely there is someone on board who can tell us where Eddie is staying," Drago suggested.

21

"The head concierge," I said. "If I can find him. Probably has an office below decks somewhere. Don't you need to get back to the castle?"

"And leave you alone to face the unknown? I don't think so. At least not until Kabita arrives and we discover what is going on. Inigo would have my scales if I let anything happen to you."

I wasn't so sure about that. "Sure. Great."

I admit I was kind of relieved he was sticking around. Normally I didn't mind being on my own, but I'd never been on a cruise ship before, and I had no idea what I was facing. Going in without any sort of backup was just plain stupid. At least I had weapons now. Back at the castle, Drago had loaned me a boot dagger and a wrist sheath knife. He'd then made arrangements for my weapons to be shipped from Paris to the castle with a promise to have Finn deliver them either to me on the ship or to my house in Portland, depending on what went down during our visit.

I had no idea where on earth to begin looking for the concierge, or if the place had a front desk like hotels. Fortunately we came across a map on the wall indicating the location of guest services.

"That's it," I said, tapping the location on the map. "They should be able to tell us how to find Eddie. I hope."

Drago nodded and took off in the direction indicated with me hurrying along in his wake. Dragons had an unerring sense of direction, one that put my inborn Hunter abilities to shame. Although the deck was fairly busy, the crowd seemed to part for Drago with ease. No one appeared conscious of it, but as he approached, people veered away, leaving a clear shot toward his goal: the elevators.

"Did you do that on purpose?" I asked as we stepped on board.

Drago punched the button for the correct deck. "Do what?" He seemed genuinely confused by my question.

"Never mind."

We rode the elevator in silence. It stopped with a ping, and the doors slid open, revealing an enormous lobby with soaring ceilings and marble floors. At one end was a long desk of polished dark wood like in those snazzy hotels. Above one end of the desk was a sign that said Guest Services.

I wasn't sure exactly how to handle this. They'd realize pretty quickly we weren't legitimate guests, and it wasn't like we could make up some random excuse for how we'd just happened to wander aboard. All I could do was play my role and hope they didn't ask me any awkward questions.

I strode across the lobby with Drago hot on my heels. The young woman behind the desk looked up at my approach, a pleasant smile plastered on her face. The smile grew wider the minute she spotted Drago. So that was how the land lay. I gave him a subtle nudge in the ribs. He wasn't stupid. He took the hint.

"Fair lady," he said, putting a little extra Highland burr into his voice and giving her a slight bow, "I would beg of you a great favor." I had to refrain from rolling my eyes.

The girl giggled and tittered. "Of course," she gushed. "I am always here to help. What can I do for you?" She eyed him like she might dive across the desk and rip his clothes off. I barely bit back a laugh.

"My sister and I are supposed to meet a friend of ours. However, she has forgotten where we are to meet." He gave her a conspiratorial look that spoke volumes about my supposed mental state. "I was wondering, could you kindly ring his room and ask him?"

There was a courtesy phone not ten steps away. I half expected her to tell him to go use it. Instead, she giggled again and said, "Of course. Do you know his room number?"

"Alas, she left it, in our room, and it is a long hike back."

They exchanged another conspiratorial look. "No worries, sir. It happens. Just give me his name, and I'll look it up for you."

He gave her a wide smile, and I thought she was going to faint dead away. "Eddie Mulligan. Although he may be booked under Edward Mulligan."

She tapped away at her keyboard. "Ah, here he is. Let me call the room." She picked up her phone and dialed. After a moment she hung up. The look she gave Drago was so mournful, I thought she might burst into tears. "I'm so sorry. He's not answering. Would you like me to leave him a message? Or perhaps I could page him?"

I stiffened. Blasting Eddie's name all over the ship was the last thing we needed. It could put him in even more danger.

"No worries, my dear," Drago said, reaching over to squeeze her hand. "You have been incredibly helpful. We will simply have to meet up with Eddie later. Come along, sister." With a little wave at the desk clerk, he ushered me back onto the elevator.

24

"How exactly was she helpful?" I hissed. "And does your wife know you're a mad flirt?"

"She won't if you don't tell her," Drago said. "Besides, it was for a good cause. When the girl dialed, I saw the room number."

I grinned. "I guess you're not just a pretty face after all."

"Be careful, or my wife will kick your ass."

Chapter Three

We found Eddie's room without much problem, and Drago "convinced" the reluctant steward to let us in. Probably he could have broken down the door just as easily, but it would have left a mess. The room was empty, and there was no sign of Eddie, only a vast amount of cravats and linen shirts littering the small space.

"Looks like the place was tossed," Drago growled.

"Uh, no. This is just Eddie. He's not exactly organized."

"Huh." He prowled the small space as if looking for clues or maybe trying to pick up a scent.

I turned to the steward, who was still dithering in the doorway. He looked like he wasn't sure whether to call security or run for his life. "Do you know where Eddie is?" I asked him.

He shook his head so hard, his glasses nearly slid off his nose. "No, ma'am. I haven't seen Mr. Mulligan in the last two days."

My eyebrows went up. "And you didn't think to tell anyone?"

"Ah, no, ma'am. You see, it's not unusual for guests not to sleep in their, ah, quarters." His tone was one of imparting a delicate piece of information. It took me a moment to get it.

"You think Eddie is shacked up with some steampunk chick?" I almost laughed at the thought. And then I remembered the crowd of women around him the last time I'd been to one of his steampunk events. Like bees to honey. Maybe it wasn't so crazy. "He never said where'd he be?"

26

"Madam. I am not in the habit of keeping tabs on our guests." He tugged on his uniform and gave a supercilious sniff. "Except, of course, when it concerns the execution of my duties."

"Listen," I said, stepping right up into his personal space. I could smell garlic on his breath. I was half tempted to offer him a mint. "Eddie called me. He said there was a problem. Something about death."

I watched him closely, but other than paling slightly as one would expect when death is mentioned, there was no other reaction. "Madam. There have been no deaths aboard that I am aware of, and certainly Mr. Mulligan would be in no danger aboard our ship." There was a hint of pride in his voice, as if this ship were superior to all other ships in the matter of passenger safety. He looked me up and down. "I cannot imagine why Mr. Mulligan would have called you. Perhaps it was his idea of a joke."

That did it. I clenched my hands into fists and started to open my mouth, but Drago caught my arm before I could let the jackass have it. "Thank you. You've been very helpful," Drago said, interrupting my pending tirade. He handed the steward a folded bill. It looked like maybe a twenty-pound note.

"Certainly, sir." The steward snatched the note and shoved it into his jacket pocket. He gave Drago a nod, me a suspicious glare, and ushered us both from the room before locking the door.

"Are there any major events today?" Drago asked.

"Major events, sir?"

"Steampunk events. Parties and whatnot."

The steward smiled. "Why, yes, sir. There is currently a costume contest. If you would come with me, I will happily give you the location."

After getting directions from the steward, Drago and I took another silent ride on the elevator. As we stepped off the elevator car, half a dozen people dressed in various states of steampunkery crowded in after us. One man wore a top hat so tall, I wondered he could get it through the elevator doors.

"We must be close," I muttered.

Drago lifted an eye brow and kept walking.

At the door to the function room, we were stopped by an overlarge man in a cowboy outfit complete with Stetson and shit-kicker boots. Only instead of a six-shooter, he had a brass and copper ray gun.

"Sorry. You're not dressed," he said, stepping in front of us. He stared us down. Well, he stared down at me, but Drago topped him by at least four inches.

"Excuse me?" I said.

"No one gets in unless they're dressed in steampunk." He said it slowly, like he thought I might be an idiot.

"Seriously?"

He crossed his arms over his chest and gave me a stern glare. With a sigh I whipped one of my knives out of the wrist sheath and held it about two inches from his nose.

"This steampunk enough for you?"

He let us in.

At the front of the room was a large stage where a Master of Ceremonies in a dark Victorian suit with one of those frilly white shirts underneath paraded about with a lot of posturing and posing. The cheap sound system crackled and popped and squealed as he announced various contestants.

"The Lady Mei Chai," he announced with a flourish.

A young Asian woman glided across the stage. Her midnight black hair was done up in a classic bun with small silver daggers stuck through in lieu of hairpins. She wore a tiny pair of round spectacles with tinted blue lenses perched on the edge of her nose, and a classic peacock-blue cheongsam – one of those gorgeous Chinese sheath dress with a mandarin collar. A dark brown waist-cincher corset showed off her tiny waist. Matching brown Victorian ankle boots and fingerless lace gloves finished off the ensemble. She posed for the crowd, twisting this way and that, showing off a pair of very nice legs through the long slits on either side of her dress. The people seated around the stage were clapping and cheering louder than the crowd at a Blazer game.

"Oh my god, I know you." The voice, about three inches from my ear, caused me to jump. The speaker was a cute little blonde wearing a top hat, a pair of brass goggles, and not a whole lot else. Tiny rhinestones marched across her high cheekbones and sparkled beneath the bright overhead lights. Her powdery perfume made my nose itch.

"Excuse me?"

"I met you this winter in Portland. The steampunk party? Eddie introduced us." I vaguely recognized her as one of the mob of women hanging around him that night. She held out her hand, "Victoria von Thistlethwaite."

"Seriously?"

She shrugged. "Well, that's who I am this week," she said with a laugh.

29

"Sure." I shook her offered hand. "Morgan Bailey."

She frowned. "That's an odd steampunk name."

"It's my real name."

"Oh." She looked somewhat disappointed. Then she brightened. "I bet you're here to see Eddie. He told me he was expecting a friend." She glanced at Drago, gave him a wide smile, and fluttered her damn lashes. I was pretty sure they were fake. Nobody had real lashes that long. When Drago didn't respond to her feminine wiles, she shrugged and turned to me. "Come on. I'll take you to him."

Victoria led the way, sashaying through the crowd like the Queen of Sheba, her pert little ass barely covered by a scrap of pink silk and a bustle thing made of olive-green mosquito netting. Or at least that's what it looked like. I'm pretty sure the fabric had some kind of fancy name, but gods knew what it was. Not my forté.

"Do you know why Eddie called me?" I asked, hurrying to keep up as she strode out into the hall. Her legs were about ten feet longer than mine.

"He didn't say. But he's been a little off the last couple of days. He's definitely hiding something, but then that's Eddie for you. Full of secrets." She paused in front of a door marked "private" and twisted the brass doorknob. "Here you go. He's been staying here. Says it's safer." She gave me a look that told me she thought Eddie was being ridiculous, then pushed open the door and popped her head in. "Eddie, that Morgan chick is here." She stepped back and waved us forward. "Have fun. I gotta get back to the contest. I'm up in a few minutes." She gave us a little finger wave and disappeared down the hall.

Drago and I exchanged glances, then with a shrug, I stepped into the room. It was clearly a storage room of some kind, but everything had been shoved against one wall. On the opposite wall hung a giant blueprint of the ship with red Xs marked in a couple of places, along with pink and yellow sticky notes covered in almost illegible handwriting. The table in the center of the room was covered in papers: long lists of names I assumed was a passenger manifest, what appeared to be background checks, and sketches of what looked like crime scene locations. Random notes in various colored ink littered the floor. Two chairs, their seats stacked high with reference books of supernaturals, were pulled up next to the table. I wondered where Eddie had gotten books in the middle of the ocean.

Eddie straightened up from where he was hunched over a file folder. "Morgan. Thank the gods. They just found another one."

"Another what?"

"Another body."

Chapter Four

"Body? What the hell is going on, Eddie?" I circled the room, stopping to stare at the blueprint on the wall. I was pretty sure the red Xs weren't party locations.

"I told you on the phone..." he began.

"The connection was horrible, Eddie. All I heard was something about death and then the line went dead."

"Perhaps we should sit down," Drago suggested. Eddie and I ignored him, so Drago shrugged and pulled out one of the chairs, dumping the books on the floor. He sank into it, propping his booted feet on the table.

Eddie sighed. "We were a day out of port when the first body showed up." He rubbed the bridge of his nose beneath his glasses. He looked tired. I could see dark circles under his eyes, and he was looking rather pasty for someone vacationing in the Bahamas.

"You found it? The body."

"Yes."

"So," I said. "Why did you call me? Why didn't you turn it over to the captain or the nearest port authorities?" I wasn't entirely clear on what the law was about bodies found at sea.

"Because the body was drained of blood."

"Shit." I cleared the other chair and took a seat, propping my elbows on the table. "So not the authorities. What about Hunters? Surely there are some in the area."

"A couple, yes. But they are inexperienced. Vampires don't exactly gravitate toward the equatorial regions. Too much sun."

"Makes sense," I said. "Okay, tell me everything."

Eddie began pacing back and forth in front of the table, hands clasped behind his back. His fringe of curly gray hair was wilder than usual, sticking out in several directions as though he'd stuck his finger in a light socket. "I came back from dinner the first evening and prepared for bed. I found the body in my shower. There was blood everywhere, but none in him."

"Let me guess. Vampire."

He nodded. "It appeared so, based on the wounds."

"Did you know him? The body, I mean."

"Not at all. He was a complete stranger. One of the cruise line employees, I believe."

"What did you do with the body?" Drago asked.

Eddie cleared his throat. "I destroyed the heart and then threw the body overboard."

"Oh, dear gods, Eddie." I buried my face in my hands.

"I didn't have much of a choice, Morgan. You know the danger better than anyone."

I did. Such an attack could mean the victim would rise from the dead a vampire. Nobody had time for that shit. Especially not on a cruise ship where the food—read: humans—were herded together like cattle. The only possible option was to destroy the heart, but that was kind of hard to explain to the authorities. Not to mention the family of the victim.

"Hasn't the ship noticed he's missing? Surely he's got friends, co-workers?"

"I imagine they have reported him missing, but so far no one has put two and two together. Hopefully they will simply assume he abandoned ship for some reason of his own." Eddie shrugged, but his eyes were bleak. I could tell he felt horrible about it, but we both knew there was nothing else he could have done.

"So, there's a vampire on board," I said.

"Clearly." Eddie removed his glasses, polished them, and put them back on. "I've done the best I can to search the ship, but I haven't had much luck."

"You said there was another body?"

"Two, in fact. The second body appeared shortly before I called you. This time there was a witness," he said grimly.

Drago and I exchanged glances. "What did you do with the witness?" Drago asked.

"Nothing. I merely convinced her she'd had a nightmare. She was rather hysterical when she woke up and found a dead body in her room. It was easy enough to persuade her."

"What was he doing in her room? Did she know him?"

Eddie shook his head. "No more than any of the rest of us. Her room is next to mine, which is why I heard the screaming. Fortunately, I arrived before the steward and was able to prevent him seeing anything untoward. I, ah, gave her a sleeping pill, and then cleaned up her room."

I was betting there had been an extra something in that sleeping pill to help along Eddie's power of suggestion. "And the body?" I asked.

"A guest this time. I'd seen him around. Something of a loner and not well liked by anyone as far as I could see. He wasn't on-board with anyone. While he may have family back home who will question his disappearance, we've got a few days before we have to worry about anything like that.

I... took care of the body. That was two days ago. I moved in here after that. It seemed safer."

"So, this third body," I said. "When did it show up?"

"Early this morning. One of the maids. I found her in this very room. How she got in, I do not know."

"Shit," I said with feeling.

"My sentiments exactly."

# # #

Kabita arrived a couple hours later by helicopter. The captain wasn't thrilled, but she flashed her Supernatural Regulatory Agency badge, and he clammed up. I'm pretty sure she lied and told him she was CIA. Nobody outside the supernatural community knew about the SRA, but nobody wanted to risk messing with a bunch of spies. Probably they'd seen too many Hollywood movies. Eddie went through the tale of the blood-drained bodies again for her benefit.

"Vampire." She spit the word out like it was a cuss word.

"Oh, yes," Eddie agreed. "Unfortunately, I've been unable to locate either it or its lair. The ship is quite large."

There was a buzzing sound. We all glanced around as if giant mosquitoes had suddenly invaded the storage room.

"That's me," Drago said, fishing his cell phone out of his pocket. He frowned as he stared at the screen.

"What is it?" I asked. "Is Inigo okay?"

"He's fine, but I am needed back at the castle. I assume you can all carry on without me." He didn't wait for an answer, but started for the door. I stopped him with a hand on his arm.

"Thank you for the lift out here."

"Of course."

Guilt was poking me in the back with a big stick. "Please watch over Inigo for me. I know I should be there, but...."

"But people are dying," he said. "You are a Hunter. It is your duty to stop the vampire responsible for this. Inigo will be fine. Just give him some time. There is nothing you can do for him right now." He gave my hand a brotherly pat and slipped out the door.

"Inigo?" I hadn't realized Kabita was standing so close.

"He's fine," I told her.

"That's good."

I gave her a look.

"That's not good?"

I sighed. "He's a bit thin and probably in need of some physical therapy to get his strength back, but physically he's fine."

"I see." There was a wealth of meaning in those two little words.

"He looks at me like I'm a stranger," I said, trying to keep the tears out of my voice. "He won't talk to me."

"I'm sorry, Morgan." She gave me a quick squeeze. "Surely Drago is right, and he just needs time."

Eddie cleared his throat. "I admit I don't know a great deal about the recovery of dragons and, as you know, Inigo is half human, which makes things a bit unusual." He polished his glasses again. "But I am quite certain he is still healing. At least mentally. It will take time. And patience. And probably a great deal more than just physical therapy."

"And in the meantime, we've got a vampire to find," I said. When in doubt, kill things. Worked for me. Besides, the faster I got this vamp business taken care of, the faster I could get back to Scotland.

Eddie showed us where on the ship he'd already searched, marking each spot with an orange highlighter. Other areas were marked with blue. "These are the areas I have not searched but which are highly unlikely to be hiding a vampire," he said, pointing to the blue marked rooms.

"Why is that?" Kabita asked. "Surely they should be checked just in case."

"Well," Eddie said with a slight smile, "this one here is a bar and all four walls are made entirely of glass."

"Ah."

"Indeed. Perfect for viewing the ocean over a tasty beverage. Not so perfect for vampires." He turned back to the blueprint and circled three places with his red marker. "These are where the bodies were found. No rhyme or reason I can see except for the obvious."

"Which is?" Kabita asked.

"They're all below decks," I said.

"Interesting. So he hasn't attacked anyone out in the open. Even at night."

"Not so far," Eddie said. "All of them have been daylight attacks."

Kabita and I glanced at each other. No regular vamp would attack a human in broad daylight. Not even below decks. They'd be holed up somewhere the sun couldn't reach them, not wandering about a busy ship where they could be easily caught. There was only one type of vampire who would risk such a thing. One type of vamp who could override their primordial fear of the sun.

"Soul vamp."

"Yes," Eddie said. "That would be my guess. For a reason unknown to us, someone has sent this vampire here for a purpose. We can only guess why."

As I stared at the blueprint, I began to see another pattern, one that confused and worried me. I had no idea what it meant. "There's one other pattern to the killings."

Kabita and Eddie stared at me. Eddie gave a slight shake of his head. "I'm afraid I can't see it."

"Can't you?" I tapped each bright red X with my forefinger. "The first body, here, was found in your shower, Eddie. The second, in the room next door to yours. And the third was right here in this very room. The room where you're trying to figure everything out." I turned back to them. "Eddie, the pattern is *you*."

# # #

Something ahead made a faint dripping sound, like a faucet that needed a new washer. There was a dank, metallic scent that tickled my nose and sat sharply on my tongue. A few caged lights gave off a dim glow, enough to interfere with my night vision but not enough to light the way.

I kept my UV gun in my hand, ready should I come face-to-face with my prey. How Eddie had gotten the thing on-board I would never know, but I was grateful for it.

We'd spent some time speculating on the reason someone would be after Eddie. It was clear that while Kabita agreed with me, Eddie was just humoring us. He clearly thought it was all one big coincidence. I had a hard time buying that, but I still couldn't figure out *why* Eddie would be part of the pattern.

The three of us spent the rest of the day searching the ship, marking off rooms as we went. At the rate we were going, it was going to take the rest of the year. After several hours we took a break. Eddie snuck us some food from the buffet, and then Kabita and I napped in his room until dark. Nighttime was always the best time for a Hunt.

After my nap I felt, if not refreshed, then at least more alert. Eddie offered to join in the hunt, but he was emceeing the steampunk ball that evening, so Kabita and I sent him on his way before heading to the place where the last body had been found. I didn't know what we hoped to find, but there wasn't anything. No clues. No residual vampire energy. Nothing.

"Listen," I said to Kabita. "A vamp's natural inclination is to go underground. The closest thing on a ship would be anything below the water line."

"Makes sense. We should concentrate our search below decks. Engine rooms. Storage bays. That sort of thing."

We'd split up and continued our search, which was how I found myself in a dim hallway somewhere in the belly of the ship. Between the bass roar of the engines and the poor lighting, I was getting a raging headache.

Somewhere deep inside me, something stirred, raising its head. The Darkness reminding me it was there, ready to be let out. If I used it, the headache would go away. I'd be able to see. The noise wouldn't bother me so much. And I'd probably find that damn vamp in half the time. But it would also bring me that much closer to the edge. To losing control for good. It wasn't worth the risk.

Then I remembered the red Xs on Eddie's wall. To prevent another murder, yes, it was worth the risk.

I took a deep breath and let the Darkness out. It surged up from that place inside me where it lived, spiraling through me and out the center of my chest. My vision narrowed to a pinprick. A point of light in a long dark tunnel. The sounds of the engines quieted. The pain throbbing at the base of my skull receded. Suddenly I could see as clearly as if it were broad daylight. I felt awake, alive, alert in a way I never did with my normal Hunter abilities.

Clenching the UV gun a little tighter, I picked up my pace as I moved down the corridor. The gripping on the back of my skull returned, but this time it wasn't a headache. I sensed the vamp. It was close.

I checked my phone. Not a single bar. No way to send Kabita a text. I was on my own.

I moved faster. The grip on my skull was growing tighter, a sure sign I was nearly on top of the thing. And then the feeling started to fade. With a frown, I stopped, turned around, and walked back a few paces. The feeling grew stronger. I should be practically on top of the vamp, but there was nothing there. Just an empty hallway. Nothing to hide behind. No doors. Nothing.

I glanced up in time to see the grate over my head come crashing down. The Darkness batted it away as if it were made of tin foil. It hit the wall with a loud clatter, leaving a dent in the panel. The vamp was another matter. It picked me up and threw me against the opposite wall. I hit so hard, I felt the metal shudder beneath me.

I brought up the UV gun, but the creature smacked it out of my hand. The gun skittered across the floor out of reach. The vamp snarled, flashing fang, eyes glowing a demonic red. It was impossible to tell if it was a man or a woman, it was so emaciated. Definitely a soul vamp. A vampire who'd had a human soul trapped within it. And it was hungry.

It slashed at me with long fingernails. I twisted to the side, narrowly avoiding having my face redecorated. I twisted around, throwing a kick that connected with the vamp's knee. I heard something snap, and the vampire tumbled to the floor with an unholy shriek. I went for my gun, but the vamp, ignoring its broken leg, leaped at me. We went down in a heap, and the thing grabbed me by the hair, smashing my head into the steel plating of the floor. Warm blood gushed from my nose.

I freed the knife from my wrist sheath and stabbed backward blindly. I must have connected, because the thing screamed and rolled away from the blade. It was enough that I was able to use its momentum to throw it off me. I rolled with it, stabbing again with my blade. I missed the heart, but it screeched enough to let me know it was hurting.

Jumping to my feet, I ran for the gun. The vamp caught my ankle, and I went down. Hard. I was pretty sure I saw stars, but the Darkness pushed back the pain, forcing me to focus. My fingers closed around the gun just as the vamp's hands closed around my throat, squeezing. I choked, gasping for air. The vamp squeezed harder. Tiny spots of black danced across my vision. The Darkness roared in anger. It wasn't about to let me die.

With every ounce of focus I could muster, I pointed the gun back over my left shoulder and gently squeezed the trigger. The vampire screamed, letting go long enough for me to suck in oxygen. A second shot, and it was off me, rolling around on the floor clutching at its face. I smelled the stench of scorched flesh. It turned my stomach, but the Darkness laughed with excitement. It liked the smell. Which only made me feel sick.

Rolling to the side, I pointed the UV gun and pulled the trigger over and over. Blast after blast of UV light hit the vamp in the chest until, between one moment and the next, it went up in flames and then exploded into dust.

The sprinklers overhead suddenly burst into action, turning me into a drowned rat. But at least it washed away the blood, both mine and the vamp's. Staggering to my feet, I tucked the gun into the waistband of my jeans and staggered toward the nearest flight of stairs. I wanted to push the Darkness back where it belonged, but I kept it with me. I needed it to overcome the pain and fatigue. It was the only way I was going to get the hell out of Dodge before I got caught.

I heard the faint sound of voices and the fall of booted feet coming my way. *Hurry*, the Darkness whispered. I ran.

Chapter Five

The minute I got to the top of the stairs, I leaned against the wall and took a deep breath, willing the Darkness back into its hole. It didn't want to go. It snapped and snarled, but slowly slunk away to that place inside me where it lived. I couldn't help the small sigh of relief. One of these days I may lose control for good, but today was not that day.

My phone had two bars, so I sent Eddie and Kabita a text: *Got him.* A couple of workmen passed me in the hall and gave me some strange looks but didn't say anything. I wasn't sure if the looks were because I was somewhere I wasn't supposed to be or because I was a hot mess.

I stared down at myself. Hot mess. For sure. I was covered from neck to toe in vamp blood. Fortunately, because vampires were technically dead, their blood was more blackish brown than red, so it looked like I'd taken a bath in motor oil. Actually, from the smell, some if it probably was motor oil.

I needed to get out of sight as quickly as possible, so I hurried toward the storage room Eddie had commandeered as his command post. The door was locked—obviously Eddie and Kabita weren't back yet—but the lock was easy enough to pick. Less than a minute, and I was inside.

I shrugged out of my stained jacket and tossed it over the back of a chair, wrinkling my nose at both the smell and the mess. I repressed a shiver. It may be hotter than the inside of a sauna above decks, but below decks, the air conditioner was cranked to North Pole levels.

There was blood splatter on my shirt, too, so I unbuttoned it and tossed it onto my jacket, leaving me in my tank top. Fortunately, that was clean. Unfortunately my boots and jeans were still filthy and I couldn't exactly run around barefoot in my underwear. At least the dark colors hid the worst of the stains. I could get back to the stateroom to clean up, put on a change of clothes. Except I hadn't brought a change of clothes.

The door swung open, and Eddie scurried in, Kabita hot on his heels. "Dear God," he said reeling back. "What is that stench?"

"Vampire blood with a light dusting of motor oil. It's very "in" this season."

Eddie frowned at my jacket and shirt draped over the chair. "Good thing you have a penchant for black. Some of those stains are never coming out. You really should change. People might notice."

"Possibly, but I don't have any other clothes."

"You got him?" Kabita asked, ignoring the byplay.

"Yeah."

"Were you able to question him?"

"He wasn't feeling very talkative." I gave them both a quick run-down on the vamp, including the fact that it was a soul vamp.

"I don't like this," Eddie said with a shake of his head. "Something feels very not right."

"You're telling me." I gathered my filthy clothes. "I'm going to take a quick shower." It would get the worst of the gunk off my skin and out of my hair.

"I will have the concierge arrange for rush laundry service," Eddie said.

"Um, great." It would be better than putting bloody clothes back on. "Then I'll put in a call to Trevor. He needs to know about this."

Eddie nodded in agreement. "That's an excellent idea. Clearly there is a reason someone set that vampire loose on this ship, and I can't imagine it was a good one."

I nodded and started to exit the room, but Eddie's voice stopped me.

"By the way, you should both get ready for the ball."

I stared first at him, then at Kabita. She shrugged. I turned back to Eddie. "What ball?"

"Why, the Grande Steampunk Ball, of course. It's the biggest event of the season, and it starts in"—he glanced at his pocket watch—"three hours. We have just enough time to eat and get ready."

"Eddie, I'm not going to a ball."

"Why not?"

"For one thing, I don't have any regular clothes to wear, never mind a ball gown."

Don't worry," he beamed. "I can fix that."

I barely repressed a groan. With my luck, I'd end up in a hoop skirt. "For another, we're here on serious business."

"And that business is completed. The vampire is dead, the immediate threat dealt with. There is nothing more we can do at the moment. We might as well enjoy ourselves."

"He's got a point." Kabita gave me a wicked grin.

I glared at them both. "Fine." I may have slammed the door a little harder than necessary.

Back in Eddie's stateroom, I stripped off my boots and jeans, then put in a call to room service. I was starving. After being assured my meal would arrive within forty minutes, I hustled my way through a shower, finishing as the food arrived. My pile of dirty clothing, including my boots, had already disappeared from the middle of the floor.

Wrapped in one of the ship's wonderfully fleecy bathrobes, I perched on the edge of the bed to enjoy my meal and make a call to Trevor. He answered on the third ring.

"Are you eating?"

I swallowed a bite of my BLT. "Yes. I'm hungry enough to eat a horse. Do you know how much energy it takes to execute a vampire?" Not to mention channel the Darkness, but I wasn't about to bring that up. I gave him an abbreviated version of events.

"You're sure it was a soul vamp?"

"Yeah. No doubt. I thought your guys destroyed all the tech." Creating a vampire imbued with a soul required a very special kind of technology, one my father had tried to destroy before his death, to no avail. Instead it had been taken for some nefarious purpose we still hadn't figured out.

"We destroyed what we could find. But it's not unlikely Alister Jones has some of it hidden away somewhere."

Alister Jones was Kabita's father, former head of MI8, the United Kingdom's version of the SRA, and a genuinely bad guy. The recent appearance of soul vampires was thanks to Alister, and I was pretty sure he'd had something to do with the death of my father as well.

"Great," I snapped. "So good ole Alister is holed up somewhere cranking out soul vamps. But why?"

"Other than the obvious?"

"His chances of creating an army of these things are pretty low now," I said. "After all, we know about the vamps and the tech. The element of surprise is gone. And with most of the tech destroyed, he can't make as many or as fast." Unless, of course, he'd found someone to recreate the technology. Which was entirely possible and very disturbing. "There's got to be more to it."

"I've no doubt of that," Trevor agreed. "I just don't know what that is right now. I've got people on it. It's the best I can do." He paused. "How are you?"

"You heard about Inigo."

He cleared his throat. "Ah, yeah. Kabita called me. She was worried about you."

"I'm fine." My voice cracked a little. "Okay, maybe fine is overstating it, but I will be fine. I'm just...he's alive, Trevor. He's healed. And yet, he's not...him. He looks at me like I'm a stranger." My throat was so tight, I could barely squeeze out the words.

"Ah, Morgan, I'm sorry." He sighed. "You probably are well aware of this, but PTSD does funny things to a person. He needs time. And treatment. Hopefully he'll come around."

"And if he doesn't?" My darkest fear given words.

"Then we'll deal with it. Together. We're family."

Family. It might be the only thing keeping me sane.

#

"You seriously expect me to wear this thing?" I stared at my reflection in the mirror, half in awe and half in horror. "I can't even move."

47

"Oh, come on, they're not that bad," Kabita said, smoothing down her lapels.

"That's because you got the good outfit," I snarled.

I didn't know how Eddie had done it, but in under an hour, he'd come up with costumes for both of us. Unfortunately, mine was an utter fail as far as I was concerned. While Kabita's costume consisted of skin tight pants, boots, and an aviator jacket—not much different from her usual clothing—mine had so many layers of bustles and petticoats and whatnot, I was half afraid I would trip and fall on my face. As if that weren't bad enough, I had to wear a full corset over a thin, silky blouse. It looked great, but I could hardly breathe, never mind move.

"This is ridiculous. I can't wear this." Every time I took a step, my skirts made a rustling sound loud enough to wake the dead.

"We're not hunting, Morgan. We're dancing." Kabita shot me a smug grin. "Now come on before we miss the ball." She grabbed me by the hand and dragged me, protesting, from the room.

"Ah, there you are. My, don't you ladies look lovely." Eddie beamed at us. He was dressed every inch the Victorian gentleman, right down to his cravat and waistcoat. Except attached to his top hat was a pair of brass goggles, and the left side of his face was decorated with a series of little metal gears. He held out his arms to both of us, which we took, and escorted us to the elevators. "Oh, this is going to be a wonderful evening. Don't you think?"

I gave him a wide, fake smile while muttering curse words in my mind. If I didn't pass out from lack of oxygen, it would be a miracle.

I had to give the organizers props. The ballroom was amazing. Swaths of fabric draped the ceiling and walls, hiding the modern fixtures from view. From the ceiling hung giant, softly glowing orbs. I had no idea how they'd done it, but it looked amazing. Magical, even. The pillars had been turned into giant steam-work pipes swathed in fairy lights. A table lit with candelabra groaned under the weight of platters of food and a bizarre brass urn that seemed to be dispensing something alcoholic. It was like something out of the Mad Hatter's tea party. A mini zeppelin whizzed about the crowd, bumping into the occasional reveler. The bumpee would laugh and grab something from the basket dangling beneath the zeppelin before it whizzed off again.

"Eddie!" A woman emerged from the crowd, arms outstretched and face wreathed in smiles.

"Now that's an outfit I could work with," I muttered to Kabita as Eddie hugged the newcomer.

The woman was not much older than me. Her long hair was almost as red as mine, but while mine came from a bottle, hers was clearly natural. Where my eyes were green, hers were gray, but we both had the pale skin that spoke of Celtic ancestry. And the curves, all of which were easy to see, thanks to her outfit.

She was dressed like something out of a Jane Austen novel, with one of those sheer cotton gowns with the high waists and tiny puff sleeves. The stays, which should have been underneath the dress, were on the outside, boosting up her ample assets like they were being offered to the world on a platter. The stays, instead of being a simple white, were made of rich blue velvet trimmed in silver. She wore simple ballet flats, and her hair was done in an elaborate Grecian style, decorated with a tiara, only instead of the expected diamonds or pearls, it was made of tiny brass gears surrounding an actual clock. Frankly, it was awesome. And a whole lot more practical for a vampire hunter. I had to remind myself I wasn't on the Hunt. I was supposed to be having fun.

"Emory," Eddie cried with delight. "You are looking lovely, as usual. Please, allow me to introduce my friends, Morgan Bailey and Kabita Jones. Ladies, this is my dear friend, Emory Chastain. She also lives in Portland."

"Lovely to meet you," Emory said with a wide, genuine smile as she shook our hands. "Any friend of Eddie's is good people."

As her hand touched mine, I felt an odd zing, almost like static electricity. The powers inside me stirred. How strange. I plastered on a fake smile, hiding my suddenly whirling mind. I was pretty sure the woman had magic, and a lot of it.

The live band struck up a tune and Emory clapped her hands. "Oh, this is my song. Gotta dance. See you guys later." And she disappeared into the crowd, gossamer skirts swirling like fairy wings. If fairies had wings, which, believe me, they didn't. I'd met the Queen of the Sidhe more times than I cared to remember. She definitely did not have wings.

We helped ourselves to glasses of spiked punch and stood back to watch the action on the ballroom floor. I had to admit, it looked like a lot of fun. The music was great. The band, dressed in kilts and top hats, rocked out on stage while the dancers made a colorful splash of movement below. I couldn't help tapping my foot to the rhythm. I finally started to relax a little.

And then the screaming started.

Chapter Six

For a split second, everything went dead quiet. The band stopped playing. People stopped dancing. I'm not even sure anyone was breathing. Then more screams rang out, and people started running. Next thing I knew, there was a stampede toward the doors.

"What the bloody hell?" Kabita shouted over the noise. She rarely swore, but the circumstances definitely called for it.

I started toward the spot where I'd first heard the screaming, only to be nearly bowled over by a man carrying an enormous gun. Probably not a real one since the thing was bigger than he was and I could make out orange plastic beneath the black paint job.

Emory pushed her way out of the crowd, eyes wide and her once white dress splattered with blood. "Eddie, come quickly." She grabbed his hand and disappeared back into the mob. Kabita and I plunged in after them, then stumbled to a halt next to Eddie and Emory.

In the middle of the ballroom floor laid the crumpled form of a woman. Her dark hair was spread out around her like a cloud, her skin icy pale. Her Victorian gown was a dark crimson touched here and there with a bit of black lace. I would have assumed she'd merely fainted except for the gaping wound at her throat and the pool of bright red blood beneath her, spreading across the hardwood floor. I could make out footprints and smears where people had skidded in the slick blood.

"What the hell happened?" I asked, staring at the body. I had a bad feeling I already knew. I knelt to take her pulse. Definitely dead. Another person in close proximity to Eddie had been killed by a vampire. The pattern was falling into place.

"Eddie," Emory's voice was barely above a whisper. "I was standing right next to her. I saw what happened. It was...." She glanced around as if to make sure no one was listening. "A vampire." She whispered the last word.

I glanced at her, startled. She knew about vampires. How? And what else did she know?

"Yes, my dear." Eddie patted Emory's hand. "That much is obvious. Why don't you run and fetch the head of security."

"Are you sure that's wise?" Kabita asked.

"I'm afraid there's no hiding it this time," Eddie said with a sigh. "Although how we shall explain this, I do not know."

"Why do we have to explain it?" I asked. "It's not like we were anywhere near the body."

"With so many eye witnesses, it's best we come up with something rather than let speculation run wild," Eddie said.

I stood up and moved closer to Emory. "Did you see the vampire?" I asked her.

She looked a little surprised. "I...ah... that is..."

"Don't worry. Morgan is a Hunter," Eddie said.

That seemed to give her relief, though I was surprised he told her. Clearly she was in the know about things supernatural. Very interesting. "Well, then, yes, I did. Clear as day. I didn't realize what he was, at first. When I saw those red, glowing eyes, I thought he was a demon."

Kabita and I glanced at each other. Soul vamp.

"He just walked up to her," Emory continued. "Grabbed her and sank his teeth into her throat right in front of everybody."

"Everything will be all right," Eddie said, patting her hand again. "Now go. Quick as you can."

With a nod, she took off running, gold slippers making a light tapping sound on the floor.

"Wonderful. Now everyone knows there's a vamp on board. We're going to have to make up a damn good cover story." Kabita scowled. Although she appeared fairly calm, her use of the simple cuss word made it clear she was anything but.

"Easy enough," Eddie murmured. "We're a theatrical lot, we steampunk enthusiasts. Perhaps we can come up with something creative and convincing. A theatrical entertainment, perhaps."

"Can we fool security, too?" I asked. "Better they don't know the truth."

"I think it's too late," Eddie murmured, nodding toward the ballroom door. I glanced over to see a man in a white uniform striding toward us, a couple of beefy guys trotting along behind him. Emory wasn't with them.

He was halfway across the floor when he stopped, turned to his men, and spoke in a low voice even I couldn't hear. The men seemed a little confused, but with shrugs went to guard the ballroom doors. The uniformed man continued toward us, his long strides eating up the floor.

He was ridiculously tall. Six foot six, I'd guess, or taller. Broad shouldered, long-limbed, and with cheekbones that could cut ice. The wheat blond hair and pale blue eyes spoke of Nordic decent, and he wore an air of authority as easily as I wore a machete. Definitely head of security.

"Mr. Mulligan," he said with a nod.

"Mr. Magnussen." Eddie nodded back.

They seemed to know each other. Interesting.

"I don't suppose I could ask you and your friends to wait outside." Magnussen had quite possibly the best poker face I'd ever seen. I couldn't quite place his faint accent.

Eddie gave him a tight smile. "I suppose you are correct. Where is Miss Chastain?"

"She was covered in evidence. I sent her to her stateroom, along with one of my female officers so she might change her clothing."

"Evidence," Eddie said tightly. "You mean blood."

Magnussen nodded and knelt beside the body. He didn't touch, simply looked. "Has anyone touched the body?"

"I did," I said, stepping forward. "Only to check her pulse and make sure she was dead." Although, of course, I'd known the moment I'd looked at her. In my line of work, you get real friendly with death. "Other than that, none of us has touched her, although what happened before we got here, I have no idea. People were running and screaming and freaking the hell out." Not that I could blame them. It must have been quite a shock watching someone rip someone else's throat out with their teeth.

"I don't think I need to roll out a major investigation. It's clear what happened here." Magnussen stood up.

"It is?" I couldn't help the surprise in my voice. I mean, of course it was clear to the rest of us, but what exactly did he think happened?

"Of course," he said, looking at each of us in turn, eyes cold and serious. "I think you have some vampire hunting to do, Miss Bailey."

# # #

"How the hell does he know what I am?" I hissed at Eddie as we hurried down the hallway toward the storage room *cum* command center.

"I will tell you in a moment," Eddie replied, pulling me behind him, Kabita striding along in our wake.

While Kabita and I had stared at the head of security in shock, he and Eddie quickly plotted a cover story to explain the latest death. They'd come up with bath salts. Not the kind you put in your water for a nice soak, but the highly illegal drug kind. It made total sense, as bath salts did crazy ass things to people. Like the guy in Florida who'd literally ripped another guy's face off with his teeth. Combine drugs with a steampunk ball, and presto chango, you've got a strung-out killer who thinks he's a vampire. Perfect cover story for the local police. After they'd settled on the story, Magnussen and his men had taken over and we were dismissed with a promise that Magnussen would meet with me later. Oh, goodie.

It would be much later, if I had my way. The guy made me strangely nervous.

Once we were inside the storage room with the door shut behind us, I whirled on Eddie. "Okay, spill. How does

Magnussen know who I am? For that matter, how does he know about vamps? And what about the other bodies? Does he know about those, too?"

"No, no. He doesn't know about the other bodies. I felt it best not to, ah, alert anyone. Unfortunately, we will probably have to tell him now."

"Okay, so the Hunter stuff? How does he know?"

"Magnussen once worked for the *Underrättelsekontoret.* The Swedish Intelligence. Much like our own CIA. For a branch similar to the SRA."

I blinked. "He was in supernatural intelligence?" That was a turn of events I hadn't expected.

"More than that." Eddie licked his lips. "Haakon Airik Magnussen is a Sunwalker."

Chapter Seven

"I'm sorry," I said. "Can you run that through the ringer again?"

"He said Magnussen is a Sunwalker," Kabita snapped. She turned to Eddie. "What the hell is he doing working head of security on a cruise ship?"

Eddie shrugged. "Who knows? Could be he still works for the *Underrättelsekontoret* and he's here undercover. Or maybe he just wanted a change of scenery."

"How old is he?" I asked.

They both stared at me. "I don't see how that is relevant," Eddie said. "But he is quite old. He was a Viking."

"A real one?"

"Well, of course. What did you think I meant? The sports team? I believe he was a friend of Erik the Red or some such. How much older he is than that, I do not know." Eddie began shuffling through the piles of documents on the table. I wasn't sure if he was actually looking for something, or trying to avoid further questions.

"And you managed to research all this?" Kabita asked, eyes narrowed. "How exactly? You can't find that stuff on the internet." She leaned one hip against the table and crossed her arms. The glare she shot Eddie was enough to make a strong man quail.

Eddie seemed to pale a little, but quail he did not. "I have been around the block once or twice, you know. I have my ways. Now, ladies, we have bigger fish to fry than Haakon Magnussen. There is yet another vampire aboard this vessel, and we must find and stop it before it kills anyone else."

I decided to allow him the subject change. At least for the moment. "I think I've finally figured out the pattern."

Eddie sighed, but Kabita raised a brow. "And that is?"

"I think someone is trying to frame Eddie for murder."

Eddie all but rolled his eyes. "That is ridiculous."

"Is it?" I asked. "Think about it. If you were investigating a series of murders in which all four deaths happened in close proximity to one man, wouldn't you be suspicious of that man? Consider him a viable suspect?"

Kabita snorted. "You'd better believe it."

"But it is clear the killer is a vampire," Eddie said. "Haakon…"

"What if the head of security wasn't a Sunwalker?" I asked. "What then? I believe it was only sheer bad luck for whoever planned this that the person investigating these crimes would be the one person who would know exactly what the perpetrator was."

Eddie sighed. "It does make a strange sort of sense, but the question is why? Why would someone care to frame me for murder?"

"Do you have any enemies?" Kabita asked. "Ones that wouldn't mind seeing you locked up?"

"None that I can think of," Eddie said. "At least none with access to the kind of technology that creates these soul-imbued vampires."

Well, that was an interesting turn of phrase. So, Eddie, the sweet, loveable guy *did* have enemies. It was hard to believe, but I'd come across stranger things.

"Maybe someone just wanted to get you out of the way for a while," I suggested.

Eddie shrugged. "I can't imagine why."

Neither could I, but I had a feeling it was important I figure it out. "In any case, we still need to find the vamp. Our best bet is to start searching where I found the other one," I said. "They must have been working together. Anything else is one coincidence too many."

"Agreed," Kabita said. "But I also think there's got to be more to it than that. There must be someone aboard controlling these guys."

"Not necessarily," I said. "Remember, soul vamps don't need to be in proximity to their creator to be controlled. Not like regular vamps. Whoever it is could be sitting on an island somewhere sipping a piña colada and getting a tan."

"We must be prepared for both possibilities," Eddie said. He leaned over, palms flat on the table, as if he was suddenly finding it hard to breathe.

"Eddie, are you okay?" I put my hand on his shoulder.

"Fine, my dear," he said, patting my hand, but his skin looked a little gray. I hadn't noticed it before, so I wasn't sure if I was imagining it or if the room just had bad lighting. "This sort of unnecessary death simply turns my stomach." He offered me a small smile. "Serving justice on this poor woman's behalf is all I need."

"Well, then that is what we will do."

# # #

While Magnussen dealt with the body and the local authorities, the rest of us headed into the belly of the ship to find the vamp. I took them straight to the spot where I'd killed the first one. It was the nature of vamps to nest together. Safety in numbers maybe. Who knew? But chances were, we'd find the second one close to where I'd dispatched the first.

We searched every inch of that damn ship from the cargo holds to the ventilation shafts. Nothing.

"He can't have just disappeared," Kabita said. "We're surrounded by water. Miles from shore."

She was right.

No wait. She was wrong.

"Shit."

Eddie and Kabita both stared at me.

"Vamps don't need to breathe," I explained as I headed upstairs to the command room.

They both stared at me as if I'd grown a second head, but followed slowly.

I sighed as I let myself into the room. "If you don't need to breathe, you don't need to worry about drowning." I let them in, then shut the door carefully. "And it takes a long time for vampires to get tired. Much longer than it would a human. He could have gone overboard. Swum as far as he could until he was either exhausted or the sun came out. Then he could have sunk to the bottom and walked to shore."

"Oh, my," said Eddie, polishing his glasses. He was looking decidedly green. I handed him a bottle of water, which he took with a grateful smile.

"You're an evil genius," Kabita said, clapping me on the back. "Though wouldn't the pressure be a problem?"

"He's dead, remember," I reminded her. "Or undead, anyway. He doesn't have to worry about getting the bends or damaging his organs or whatever."

"So, how do we find him?"

"That might be a little more complicated." I unrolled a map across the table. "The nearest island is here." I stabbed at it with my finger. "But as far as I can tell, it's really small and completely uninhabited."

"Perfect place to hide," Eddie speculated, sinking into a chair at the head of the table. He was looking better, but he was still a little off-color.

"Except he's a vampire. Where would he hide from the sun? There are no buildings and trees won't cut it."

"Wade back out to sea?" Eddie suggested.

"Possible, but a pain in the ass. My guess is he's headed toward his maker or whoever has control over him. Whoever the creator is, I doubt he — or she — is going to hang out on a tiny empty island. If I were a true evil genius, I'd be hanging out on the beach sucking down frosty beverages." I stabbed at another island. "Here maybe. It's big enough to have a comfortable resort and all the creature comforts. Or here." I tapped my finger on another one. "A little small and rustic, but possible."

"I can call back the helicopter," Kabita suggested. "Easy enough to check out those islands."

"I doubt the captain is going to let you land a helicopter on deck again," Eddie pointed out. "Not without some explanation, which we can't give him. If he gets involved in this investigation, he's going to want to hold you as material witnesses. Possibly turn you over to the authorities."

"We can't afford that kind of delay," I said. "We need to get off this boat and to those islands as quickly as possible."

"Maybe we can take one of the lifeboats," Kabita suggested. "Or the wave runners. They've got some down below."

Eddie shook his head. "They will catch you quite easily, I'm afraid. They tend to keep an eye on such equipment, and there is no way you can launch without the bridge being notified and assuming, quite correctly, that the vehicles are being stolen."

I gave a frustrated sigh. "How then? Every minute we're on this ship is another minute wasted. We can't lose this vamp. He's our only lead to whoever is controlling him."

"I might, ah, be able to help you with that," Eddie said.

Kabita and I glanced at each other. "We're listening."

"It's a bit unconventional, and you'll both get quite wet, but I think I know someone who can help."

Chapter Eight

Eddie insisted we wait for full dark to carry out "the plan," but he refused to tell us what he had up his sleeve or who he'd found to help. Instead he handed us the key to his stateroom and shooed us off with the order to rest before disappearing toward the elevators.

"I don't know about you," Kabita said as she paced the narrow strip of floor next to the table, "but I am way too keyed up to sleep. Want to hit the casino?"

I shook my head. "I feel like I haven't slept in days. I'm going to do what Eddie suggested and take a nap."

Kabita nodded. "Meet you in a couple hours," she said before striding down the hall after Eddie.

I locked up behind me and headed in the opposite direction. Once in Eddie's room, I pulled the heavy drapes over the window, kicked off my boots, and threw myself on the bed. The bed was large and plush, and smelled of salt and sea. I was out within seconds.

###

Lush green grass as tall as my waist brushed me as I passed, tickling where it touched bare skin. The snug leather leggings I wore felt strange and a little too warm for the fine weather of this land, but they were practical. The short matching leather bodice bound my breasts tightly in place while allowing freedom of movement. I had been wearing a woolen tunic over the top, but it was far too hot, so I'd stuffed it in my pack and went about with stomach and arms bared. No one minded. In fact, most of the other women were dressed the same.

I started. Other women?

A quick glance around the wide grassy plain revealed a dozen other women in clothing much like mine, hair either shaved close to the skull or bound in braids. There were no men. Instead, the women were clearly warriors. Weapons bristled from their belts and packs: swords, daggers, bows. It was as though they expected to be attacked at any moment. We moved at a fast pace, wading through the endless sea of grass, headed toward... what? I had no idea.

We crested a rise, and the woman who was clearly our leader raised her hand. The entire company came to a halt. Below us spread a vast water. It had waves, like an ocean, but the air lacked the briny tang of salt. A lake then, and freshwater, too. Large enough I couldn't see the end of it. One could easily lose a ship out there.

The leader turned to face me, her dark eyes circled with fatigue. "Princess," she said, "we are here."

But where was "here?"

###

I woke to Kabita pounding on my door. I stumbled out of bed and staggered across the floor to let her in. I nearly broke my ankle tripping on my boots.

"Come on. Time to go."

"Give me a sec," I said, limping to the bathroom to use the facilities. As I splashed my face with cold water, the dream played over in my mind. This wasn't the first time I'd dreamed of being the Princess. The first time, she'd been a small child escaping from the dying city of Atlantis. The second time, she'd been a teenager running from the Temple of the Moon and invaders who were slaughtering the priestesses. She had been with the High Priestess called Amaza, and they'd been running for a distant colony. In this dream the Princess had been older. Closer to twenty, maybe. But where was she? And why was the dream so damned important?

# # #

"You have got to be kidding me." Kabita hung half over the railing, a large flashlight trained below as she stared at the water with a frown. I wasn't sure if she was talking about the long drop to the ocean's dark surface or what was waiting for us below. Either way, I couldn't blame her. Now that it was full dark, we could finally put our plan into action. Unfortunately the plan didn't help ease my mind one bit.

"No kidding. Eddie," I said, turning around to face him. "You don't think we're going to jump, do you?"

"Of course, my dear." Eddie beamed. "How else do you expect to get down there? It is the most expeditious way I could think of."

I glanced over the rail again and shuddered. It wasn't that I had a heights problem. It was that I had a jumping-off-a-perfectly-good-deck problem. Especially when the seething cauldron I was supposed to land in was a good twenty or so feet below. "And the, ah, creature waiting for us?"

Eddie joined us at the railing and peered over. The wind whipped his halo of gray hair into a froth of wild curls. "Perfectly harmless, I assure you. And an excellent swimmer. If he can pull Poseidon's damned chariot around, he can certainly carry the two of you to shore."

"Make that three," said a deep voice behind us.

All three of us whirled around to find Haakon Magnussen looming over us like an avenging Viking angel. Good gods, he was tall. Taller even than Jack, and Jack wasn't exactly a shrimp. In the darkness his hair practically glowed, but his eyes were dark unreadable slits. Still, I didn't need to read his eyes to feel the anger and determination rolling off him.

"Oh, no, my dear boy," Eddie said, thrusting his hands into his pockets and drawing himself up to his full height. All of about five feet. "You couldn't possibly ride along with the girls. They have a job to do, as do you. And yours is here on the ship." He gave Magnussen a stern, almost fatherly glare. Magnussen ignored him.

"You know very well why I must go with them," Magnussen said. His English had a slightly stilted quality to it. Almost overly proper like many non-native speakers. Except he spoke it with an almost perfect West Coast American accent. Interesting.

Eddie sighed. "Fine. The Hippocampus can take you too. If you insist."

"I do."

"Hippocampus," I muttered to Kabita. "Isn't that part of the brain?"

She rolled her eyes. "Didn't you study Greek mythology in school?"

I shrugged. "Sure, but I've been kinda busy since then. Creatures from Greek mythology haven't been exactly high on the priority list."

"Well, that down there is a Hippocampus," she said, pointing over the railing, "and according to mythology, two of them pull Poseidon's chariot around his underwater kingdom."

"So Poseidon is real, I guess." He wouldn't be the first god I'd discovered was more than an ancient myth. It still never ceased to amaze me.

"Yep."

"Huh." I stared down at the creature waiting for us. The front half was a horse. A very large, very powerful horse. Clydesdale maybe, or something bigger. The back half was something else entirely. It was fish-like in that it had scales and fins, but it was long and sinuous like I'd always imagined a sea serpent would be. It was too dark to make out any color, but its scales shimmered slightly in the lights from the ship. "And we're supposed to ride that thing?"

"More like let it pull us through the ocean. Like riding a dolphin."

"I did not sign up for this shit."

"Ladies," Eddie interrupted. "You really must get going. The Hippocampus needs to take you to shore and return to Poseidon's palace before dawn." He gave a shooing motion as if to hurry us along. How in Hades had I managed to get myself into this?

Oh, yeah. It was my job.

"Here," I said, unclasping the Atlantean amulet that always hung around my neck and handing it to Eddie. "Hang on to this for me. Don't want it ending up at the bottom of the ocean."

"Hmm. Yes. Can you imagine if Poseidon got his hands on it? He's already insufferable enough. Don't worry. I'll take good care of it."

I clambered up and over the railing until my feet were braced on the deck on the ocean side while my hands gripped the railing behind me. We were on the lowest exposed deck, but it was still way too high if you asked me.

"Here goes nothing."

I leapt into space, arching out over the water, and then the water was rushing toward me. I hit hard, plummeting beneath the surface for several yards before I started to slow. I began to kick my way to the surface, but the motion of the giant ship above me churned the water so I tumbled sideways, losing my sense of place. Panic threatened to overwhelm me. I couldn't find my way to the top, and I was running out of air. I flailed uselessly, my lungs burning. And then the weirdest thing happened.

It was like the ocean currents themselves changed course, pushing me toward the surface. Suddenly I popped up out of the water and dragged in deep lungsful of salty air. I half expected to get hit in the face with waves, but I didn't. It was as if the ocean itself held me up out of the water. I really must be losing it. Lack of oxygen to the brain for sure. How many brain cells had I lost this time?

Then the Hippocampus appeared beside me, whickering softly and nudging me with his velvety nose. I wrapped one arm around his massive neck, tangling my hand in his thick, silky mane. With the other I gave him a good nose rub, which earned me another gentle nudge.

Raising his head, the massive creature began swimming through the water, front legs churning up foam while the serpentine tail propelled us at the most unbelievable speed. I grabbed his mane with both hands and hung on for dear life, letting myself be dragged through the ocean like a rag doll.

We pulled up alongside Kabita, who was calmly treading water as if she ended up in the middle of the ocean every day of her life. She gave the Hippocampus a nose rub, and he whickered some more. Then she used his mane to lever herself up so she was straddling his back like she was on a proper horse.

"I thought you said we had to ride him like a dolphin," I said, pushing a strand of soaked hair out of my eyes.

"Apparently he wants the two of us to ride astride. Magnussen will have to do the dolphin thing."

"What? You can talk to him now?"

She smirked. "No. Eddie can."

"He and I are going to be having words later." I reached up, and she helped me haul my ass on board while the Hippocampus waited patiently. As soon as I was on, he swam toward a third figure in the water. Magnussen was already plowing through the waves toward us with long, even strokes. Clearly he and the water got along just fine.

The ship had nearly disappeared into the darkness by the time we were all aboard the Hippocampus. The creature wheeled and took off for the nearest island at top speed as if carrying two normal humans and one massive one was all in a day's work.

Chapter Nine

The hippocampus sliced through the water, legs churning up foam in front of him. It was a good thing we were doing this at night. I'd hate to have to try and explain our ride to the harbor patrol. I was having a hard enough time trying to explain it to myself, and I was used to weird things.

Our ride dropped us off on a deserted beach on the least populated side of the second island from the charts. Then he turned around and charged back into the sea, disappearing beneath the waves.

"Well," Kabita said, wiping salt water off her face, "that was different."

"No shit." I stared at the deserted beach. I couldn't see anything but the faint glow of pale sand and the dark outlines of palm trees. No lights from a nearby house or headlights from cars passing by the beach. There was absolutely no sign of human life. No sign of vampire life, either, if the lack of pain in the back of my skull was anything to go by. "Why did he drop us off here? Other than obviously not wanting to be seen, I mean."

"This was the nearest point of populated land to the ship at the time the vamp went overboard," Magnussen said, voice cool, face impassive. "Couple that with this being a low populated area, it seemed the most logical place to start."

"Okay, Mr. Spock," I snarked under my breath.

A smile twitched the corner of his mouth. "You can call me Haakon."

71

"Uh, sure thing. Haakon." I pronounced it "Haw-ken" which wasn't quite correct, but I couldn't seem to get my mouth to form the vowels properly. He winced.

"Close enough."

"Now, how are we going to find this vampire?" Kabita interrupted as she finished wringing seawater out of her long, thick braid. "This is a pretty big island. The vamp could be anywhere."

"I can't sense him," I admitted. "And he's got at least an eighteen-hour head start on us. Even if he landed on this very beach, he could be on the other side of the island by now."

"If we are correct and he is headed toward whomever is controlling him," Magnussen—er, Haakon—said. "I would think it unlikely such a person would reside in the center of town or any other heavily populated area."

I shrugged. "Depends on if the vamp's master is a people person or not." Or was human or not. But I didn't mention that out loud. I figured I didn't need to. "Let's find a road. There must be one nearby. We can figure it out from there."

The three of us trudged across the beach toward the dark silhouettes of palm trees waving in the sea breeze. The sand shifted constantly under my boots, making walking difficult. My legs burned with the effort. Kabita and Haakon had out their flashlights, but I didn't bother. I could see better without one. One of the more positive side-effects of channeling just a touch of the Darkness.

I scanned the line of trees for a path leading off the beach. I finally found an area where the foliage seemed marginally less dense than the surrounding underbrush. I led the way through, stopping short as something caught my eye. Streaks of something dark glimmered on a low hanging branch. I'd have never seen it if it hadn't been for my extra-special night vision. I stepped closer, sniffing. I caught the faintest hint of copper and decay. Vampire blood. Idiot had gotten himself sideswiped by a low-hanging branch.

"We're in the right place," I told the others. Without waiting for a response, I pushed my way quickly through the brush, scanning intently for more signs the vamp had been there. Without my bidding, the Darkness rose. My vision tunneled down to a pinprick of light against a field of black. Suddenly it was as if a path was laid out before me: a smear of blood here, a strand of hair there. Each object was surrounded by a slight purple glow as if the Darkness was saying, "Here you go." Yes, the vamp had definitely come this way.

I heard the others following me, but I was completely focused on the task at hand. Like a bloodhound, the Darkness inside me eagerly hunted down each little glowing drop of blood. I had no idea why my vision saw the drops as luminescent. The blood itself was long dried even in the humid air of the tropical island. But whatever it was, the Darkness was pulling at the leash, eager to chase it down.

I finally stumbled out onto a narrow dirt road just wide enough for a car to squeeze between the trees on either side. The trail of blood drops stopped. "Damnit," I snarled under my breath. The Darkness snarled something worse. I mentally told it to shut up. It sulked.

"What is it?" Kabita asked, pushing her way out onto the road, her breathing heavy, Haakon hot on her tail. She

73

glanced up and down the road as if expecting a vamp to come charging out of the night.

"The trail ends here," I told her. "He must have gotten into a car." It was the only thing that explained the abrupt end of his trail.

"We'll never find him." Kabita was clearly not thrilled with the idea. "If he got in a car, he could be miles away."

"Maybe not," Haakon said.

We both stared at him. "What do you mean?" I asked.

"There may be a way to track him." He pulled something out of his pocket. It was a plastic bag shaped like a walkie-talkie. He ripped open the sealed packaging and pulled out a satellite phone.

"Nifty," Kabita said as Haakon began pressing buttons. "I should get you one of those." She shot me a sideways glance. "Then you'd have no excuse not to answer my calls."

"Hey, the last time I was underground," I snapped. "Pretty sure those things don't work in tunnels."

She just gave me The Look, which I ignored. We both turned our attention to Haakon, who was barking orders into the sat phone in a language I didn't recognize. It sounded vaguely European. I'd bet it was a Scandinavian language. Maybe his mother tongue, whatever that was. Norwegian or Swedish maybe. What language had Vikings spoken, anyway? I was going to have to look that up.

"All right," Haakon said as he hung up. "Let's go." He started walking down the road toward the dark mountains looming in the distance.

"Why that way?" I trotted along behind, trying to keep up with his damn long-legged stride.

"This is the way the car went."

"And how do you know that?"

"I've got my sources."

Kabita and I exchanged looks. I glanced up at the sky. "Let me guess. You've got somebody who can access satellite images."

He raised an eyebrow. "So, you're not just a pretty face."

"Don't be an ass. You know what I am."

He smiled a little at that. "As you know what I am, I imagine."

"Eddie told me," I admitted. "But I probably would have figured it out."

"Eventually," Kabita said dryly. I shot her a dirty look.

Haakon said nothing, but there were definite signs of a smirk as we continued down the road. Or rather, he continued walking. Kabita and I were closer to a jog. I subtly tapped into the Darkness, channeling just enough to keep me from getting tired. Oddly enough, it cooperated without throwing much of a snit. My, my, what a cooperative little superpower.

I wanted to ask Haakon about the whole Sunwalker thing. The only Sunwalker I'd ever met was Jack—well, and supposedly me, but I liked to ignore that little factoid—and the only thing I knew about them was what little Jack had told me. And what I'd learned from my dreams and Eddie's sentient book. Maybe Haakon would know more or at least be willing to share. I also had a *lot* of questions about the whole Viking thing. Because, frankly, Vikings were awesome. But first, we had a vampire to stake.

# # #

It felt like days later, but was probably only about an hour, when we finally reached the edge of civilization. Low houses gleamed white in the moonlight, their windows like dark, empty eyes. There were no streetlights, only the occasional security light left burning over a garage or front door. A dog barked sleepily nearby, answered by another. I heard what I could have sworn sounded like a goat. Other than that, it was nothing but us and the crickets.

The dirt road turned to gravel and finally pavement. Although the asphalt was so pitted and scarred, "paved" could only be used in the loosest sense of the word. The houses grew closer together and eventually the odd streetlight sprung up here and there, though half of them were out. Finally we found ourselves standing in the middle of a village. Well, village was maybe too enthusiastic. They didn't even have a traffic light. Just a beat-up stop sign where two roads converged with a shop on one corner and a cafe/bar on another.

"The vamp came here?" I couldn't keep the incredulity from my tone, but seriously, this wasn't the kind of place vampires usually hung out. It was both too remote and not remote enough. In such a small community, people tended to notice when their neighbors started getting snacked on.

"This is where the car dropped him off." Haakon propped his hands on his hips and glared around him as if the village would spit up its secrets. A rooster crowed in the distance.

"Okay, so where did he go after that?" I asked, glancing around as if I might catch sight of our prey. Unlikely. The sky

76

was starting to turn gray, which meant the vamp had gone to ground. If he was smart.

"No idea," Haakon admitted.

"What? Your fancy schmancy satellite whatsis couldn't tell you that?"

He glared at me. "It could have, but my guy had to get off the system before he got caught."

"Enough, you two," Kabita interrupted our spat. "This isn't helping. Let's split up and see if we can find any sign of the vampire."

"Good plan, but you and I left our phones back on the ship," I said. We didn't have Haakon's fancy little plastic pouch and there hadn't been time to hunt down a Ziploc. "How are we going to let each other know if we find what we're looking for?"

"Sun's coming up. The vamp isn't going anywhere," Kabita said. "So, we meet back here in one hour."

I didn't bother pointing out that since I didn't have my phone, I also couldn't tell time. No watch. It didn't matter. The town was so small, it wouldn't take even close to an hour to search it. I nodded in agreement.

"I'll take the east side," Kabita said, nodding toward the side of the street with the market.

"I'll go west." Haakon moved off toward the cafe/bar.

"I guess that leaves north for me since there's nothing south. We would have seen it." But I was talking to myself. The others had already disappeared into the pre-dawn gloom.

I continued along the main street running through town. Beyond the market and bar, more of the low cinder-block houses marched neatly on either side of the road.

Narrow dirt tracks crossed the street in a couple places, creating haphazard blocks. About three blocks from the intersection stood a lonely one-pump gas station that had seen better days. A hand-painted sign noting the price of gas leaned against the side of the building. By my calculations, it was in the neighborhood of five dollars per gallon. Holy crap.

Past the gas station, the houses thinned out, the lots growing increasingly larger until we were back to jungle. After a while I stopped walking. I'd gotten no sense the vamp was near and there was no way to tell where he might have gone. I turned around and walked back into town until I came to the first dirt crossroad. There was no street sign to tell me the name, just a track headed east, disappearing between two houses. On the west side, the dirt track was even narrower. More like a trail. My guess was it led to the ocean. I took the road on the east side.

A cat glared at me from its precarious perch on the fence post next to the road. It blinked glowing yellow eyes and flashed a bit of fang. I wondered if it sensed the Darkness in me, or if it didn't like people in general.

Ignoring the cat I moved farther down the road between a second pair of houses. These faced the dirt road instead of the main street. In one, a light glowed in the front room, so I hurried by as quickly as possible. The last thing we needed was to get the locals riled up about strangers lurking in their yards.

A few more feet, and the road dead-ended onto a second dirt track running parallel to the main road. This one was slightly wider, big enough for a small car to pass, as if someone planned to pave it in the future but hadn't gotten around to it yet. Potholes had been filled in with pebbles and sand, making walking marginally easier. Like the main street, this one was lined with cinder-block houses in varying states of disrepair. Clearly the town was not on the tourist map, and it showed. Either people didn't have the money to fix up their houses, or they didn't care.

I still hadn't caught any sign the vamp was nearby. There was only so far it could or would walk, especially since it had been close to daylight when it hit shore. It would have gone underground somewhere nearby. Of course, it could have left at nightfall. It would have had several hours to get out of town before we arrived. I sighed. Might as well check the north end of the street while I was here.

I walked past more of the cinder block houses with more of the same overgrown yards studded with fruit and palm trees. The thick air was fragrant with the scent of frangipani and other tropical flowers. I really wished I was here on vacation. And that Inigo was here with me.

I shoved that thought down ruthlessly. Thinking about Inigo would only take my mind off the task at hand and send me tumbling down a very dark hole. I needed to stay focused.

I was nearly to the end of the street, about to turn back, when I felt a little tingle at the base of my skull, so faint I nearly missed it. The street was a dead end, no driveways or anything to indicate houses deeper in the jungle. I frowned, moving to one side of the street and then the other. The tingle was stronger on the east side, definitely. Stepping off the road, I moved cautiously through the heavy undergrowth. The tingle grew stronger, turning into an outright painful grip on the back of my skull. The vampire was close.

Branches and vines swiped at my bare arms. I wished for my jacket, but I'd left it back on the ship. I hadn't wanted it to get ruined by the sea water. Besides, it was far too hot for a coat of any kind, despite what Haakon seemed to think. I winced as another branch slapped my arm, raising a welt, no doubt.

At last I broke into a small clearing just as the sky above was lightening, and the horizon was turning pink. The grip on my skull was fierce now. I had to be right on top of him.

In the center of the clearing stood what looked like a garden shed made of cinder block with a corrugated tin roof. The building had been painted green, like the jungle around it, including the roof and door. There were no windows. It was a bit small, but it was a perfect place for a vampire to hide from the sun. Behind the shed swelled a small hill thick with trees. We were in the foothills of the mountains.

A smile quirked my lips as I strode toward the shed. It was probably close to the hour mark, but I didn't care. That vamp and I were going to have it out here and now. I was going to get the info I needed, and then I was going to dust the asshole. Kabita and Haakon could just wait.

Gripping the brass doorknob, I gave it a twist. It turned easily, but the door didn't open. I gave it a good shake, but it didn't budge. I bit out a curse. Deadbolt, of course. From the inside. I felt the door. It wasn't metal, which was good. Harder to burn metal. Unfortunately it wasn't wood, either, which would have been easy to either kick open or burn down. It was some man-made resin shit. I gave it a half-hearted kick. No way that thing was coming down easy. I'd have to burn it. If it could burn without killing me from the fumes. I laid my palm flat against the door, closed my eyes, and willed the Fire inside me to rise.

"What in Valhalla do you think you're doing?"

I spun around with a yelp, tiny sparks jumping from the tips of my fingers. Haakon stood a few paces behind me, glaring, arms crossed over his massive chest.

"I'm opening this door," I said. "The vamp's in there."

"You were supposed to come meet us."

"I had better things to do. How did you find me?"

He gave me a look I couldn't quite interpret. Instead of answering, he strode toward the door, nudged me out of the way, and did the same twist-jiggle thing I'd tried.

"It's bolted from the inside," I informed him in my haughtiest tone.

He didn't exactly roll his eyes, but I swear I could feel him doing it in his head. "Stand back."

"Really?" I propped my hands on my hips. "Who do you think you are? Thor?"

"Do I look like I make a habit of carrying power tools? Stand back."

With a sneer, I moved back a few paces. "Have at it."

"Thank you, kind lady. You are too good to me." Now who was the one being snarky?

Haakon rolled his shoulders, stretched his neck from side to side, and then gave his knuckles a good crack. Was he going to punch the door? He'd break his hand for sure.

He drew one leg up and let go a kick that would have done a ninja proud. The door flew off its hinges and crashed against the opposite wall before slamming to the floor of the shed, sending up a small cloud of dust. It all happened so fast, I barely had time to blink.

"Show off," I muttered.

Haakon gave me a serene smile. "After you."

"Such a gentleman." Thank gods he wasn't like Jack, insisting on going first. Never mind I was the expert on vampires. Hunting them anyway.

I wondered what waited for us beyond that doorway. I would have given anything for a UV gun or my machete, but all I had was a knife. I smiled a little. And my powers. I didn't like using them if I didn't have to, but they came in handy at times like these.

Cautiously, I poked my head through the open doorway. All I could see was the inside of an empty shed. Other than a few cobwebs hanging from the ceiling and a dirt floor, there was nothing. Except I could still feel that tightness gripping the back of my skull. There was definitely a vamp nearby.

I stepped through the doorway and paced the small room. Nothing.

"Anything?" Haakon's head appeared around the doorjamb.

"No...." I frowned. "Wait a minute." I paced back across the small space. Yes. Something was definitely off. One side of the shed floor felt and sounded like a dirt floor should: solid. The other side, however, had a slightly hollow sound as I walked across it. And it felt—I pushed down with my right foot—yes, there was definitely a slight give. "There's something here."

Haakon joined me, his massive frame taking up most of the small space. He knelt down and brushed the palm of his hand over the dirt. "I think there's a trapdoor here."

I stepped back and let him scrape away at the dirt with his hands. Sure enough, there was the outline of a door.

"The vamp's down there," I said. I had no doubt it was true. The pain in my head hadn't gone away.

Haakon nodded. "He didn't cover this door himself. He had to have had help." He didn't say it, but I knew he meant help of the human variety.

"I'm guessing his maker."

Haakon frowned. "Another vamp wouldn't have risked getting caught in daylight."

"I mean his human maker."

He gave me a look that said I'd clearly lost my mind. "What are you talking about?"

"Tell you later. Right now we've got a vamp to dust."

# # #

Beneath the trapdoor a rough ladder made of two-by-fours stretched down into the darkness. Unfortunately, it didn't stretch quite as far as I would have liked. The space under the shed floor couldn't have been more than about four feet high. It was hardly more than a crawlspace. Claustrophobia reared its ugly head. What was with me and all this underground nonsense lately? I'd had more than my fill beneath the streets of Paris.

Taking a deep breath, I descended the ladder into the tight space. Before crouching to fit beneath the floor, I slid my knife from the sheath in my boot. I still had my wrist sheaths as backup, but there was no way I'd be able to get a knife out of my boot in that small space. How Haakon was going to fit, I had no idea. I had even less of an idea how I was going to fight a vampire with so little room.

The smell of damp earth tickled my nose. I squatted, placing my left hand flat on the bare earth for balance. That was all it took. Deep within me my Earth power stirred, unfurling like a vine reaching for the sun. Of all my powers, it was the newest and least under control. Without my bidding, it seeped out of my pores, shimmering over my skin like a green mist. All around me plants began to sprout from the dirt, never mind we were underground and away from sunlight.

"What the hell?" I hadn't realized Haakon was so close behind me. "Is that you?"

"Umm...." How to explain this? "Sort of."

"Well, stop it. The last thing we need is to be fighting weeds *and* a vampire."

I was about to comply when I noticed something. The plants around me shimmered with the same greenish light as my skin. I'd expected it to end in a wall about the same place as the shed wall above us, but it didn't. The shimmer of green continued several feet into the darkness.

"Haakon, this isn't just a hole. I think this is a tunnel."

"Wonderful." He sounded about as thrilled as I felt.

"Come on, big boy. Let's see where this leads."

# # #

Leaves and flowers tickled my bare arms and face as I crawled through the near blackness of the tunnel. I'd managed to shove my Earth power back down where it belonged, but the plants themselves—the plants I'd made grow underground—still gave off a strange green luminescence. Thank goodness, because I wasn't sure even my superior night vision could have seen anything down here.

My knees were sore, and my palms stung from sharp rocks liberally scattered in the dirt of the tunnel. It was hot and sticky and far too close for comfort. My heart pounded in my ears, my breath coming in short gasps. I was close to a full-blown panic attack, which was sort of embarrassing to admit, even to myself. Hunters were supposed to be fearless. Clearly my brain hadn't gotten the memo.

I sensed Haakon close behind me. I couldn't imagine how he was doing. He was far bigger than me. It was a wonder he even fit in the tunnel.

Up ahead I saw where the shimmer of green ended in a gaping hole of black. "I think we're close," I whispered. Haakon tapped my boot to let me know he'd heard. I took a deep breath and crawled the last couple of feet.

The darkness was so complete, I couldn't see a thing. There was no green shimmer of light from plants. Even my night vision wasn't working. I cautiously stood up. My head didn't hit anything.

"You can stand up," I whispered. "At least I can."

There was silence for a moment. "Me, too. We didn't angle down, so we must be under a hill."

The hill behind the shed. Clearly someone had taken advantage of that little quirk of the landscape. "You got a light? I didn't exactly come prepared for underground exploration."

"One moment." There was a rustling sound followed by a snap, and then a dim, bluish light filled the space. Haakon held the glow stick high. We were standing inside what looked like a large, underground dome made of carefully placed rocks. And from the ceiling....

"Holy shit," I breathed, staring at the seething mass.

"You got that right."

We hadn't just found a vampire. We'd found a whole damn nest.

Chapter Ten

"Oh, hells bells, this is so not good," I hissed. "There are way too many of them. Where the hell is Kabita when you need her?"

Haakon didn't answer me. Probably realized my question was entirely rhetorical. "Looks like at least half a dozen. Maybe more."

Great. I'd handled that many before, but not on my own. I'd always had Jack. Or Inigo. I shoved that thought ruthlessly aside. Haakon would have to do. He was a Sunwalker, after all. And if Eddie was right, a former Viking. I was pretty sure he'd know a move or two. I stared at the knife in my hand. Damn, I could really use a machete right about now.

I had something else, though. Something most Hunters didn't have. Something that was far more deadly than a blade. I had Fire.

"Um, you might see something kinda weird," I told him.

"You mean weirder than you glowing green and making flowers sprout out of the dirt?"

"Possibly."

He gave me a look. "Fantastic."

"Just don't freak, okay?"

"I am not in the habit of 'freaking,'" he said stiffly.

All righty then.

With my eyes still fixed on the ceiling and the mass of hibernating vampires, I reached down into that place where my powers dwelled. They raised their heads, eager to get out. Smoke twined around Fire. Earth shimmered with green. Under them all was the black, roiling mass of Darkness. I frowned. Beneath the Darkness, lurking just out of sight, I could have sworn I sensed something else. Something new. I shook my head. I must be losing it.

Refocusing my energy, I coaxed Fire from its lair. I didn't have to work too hard. It surged out of me, flame spreading down my left hand like a fiery glove.

"Holy shit," Haakon echoed my sentiment from earlier.

"Told you."

We didn't have time to discuss it any further. The vamps above our heads began to stir.

I tightened my grip on the knife, fervently wishing I had one of Tessalah's flash bang grenades. They were like the regular flash bangs the army used, but with a little extra UV juice. Enough to disable the entire nest. Heck, at this point I'd take a plain old gun with plain old bullets. I wiggled my fingers a little, the flame dancing merrily in the dark. I'd have to make do.

I glanced at Haakon. He had a blade in one hand and a gun in the other.

"How the hell...?" He lifted an eyebrow. I shook my head. "Never mind." I might have known he'd have a way to keep a UV gun operational underwater. I was going to have a talk with Tessalah after this. If I survived. The Fire inside me laughed.

The first vamp peeled off the ceiling and dropped to the floor. The scent of death and decay stung my nose. I knew I wasn't really smelling it. To an ordinary human, a vamp smelled no different than anyone else, but my Hunter senses allowed me to smell the monster beneath the thin veneer of normal.

The vamp hissed at us, flashing long, yellowed fangs.

"Its eyes are red." Haakon sounded stunned.

"A human is in control of the nest." Normally a vampire nest was controlled by the strongest vamp, but once in a while a human used otherworldly means to gain power over a nest. In those cases, the entire nest's eyes turned red. I had no idea why.

"Shit."

I braced myself as the vampire rushed us, but it was Haakon who took it out. One shot from his UV gun, and the beam drilled a smoking hole in the vamp's brain. The thing dropped in its tracks like something out of a zombie movie. There was a howl from above and three more vamps dropped to the floor, followed by a fourth.

Another shot from Haakon's gun drilled through the breast of one of the vamps, taking out the heart. It burst into dust. And then the rest of them were on us.

One of the vamps flew at me, long hair whirling about her face. I knew it was a female only because she was half-naked from the waist up. Not out of sexiness, but because; her clothes had practically rotted off her. She was old. Really old. Definitely not a soul vamp, but still controlled by a human.

She slashed at me with long, ragged fingernails. I punched her in the jaw with my left hand. Honestly, it barely grazed her, but the fire singed her skin black from jaw to cheekbone. She screeched in pain and anger, leaping back. I gathered the Fire in my hand and hurled it through the air like a baseball. She dodged the flame, sneering at me as it splatted against the rock wall and sizzled out.

She came at me again, but this time her eyes were on my left hand as she weaved slightly to make a more difficult target. Clever minx. Maybe someone was at home in there after all. She was so busy watching my left hand, she forgot about my right. I slashed out with the knife, the sharp blade parting the skin along the side of her throat nearly to the bone. Black blood spilled over what remained of her clothing, her screech this time more of a gurgle. She stared at me in shock. Her hesitation was all I needed. I threw another fireball straight at her chest. She exploded in a cloud of dust.

I didn't have time to celebrate as another two vamps were on me. I had no idea what was happening with Haakon, and I didn't have time to check. I was too busy fending off my own attackers.

One came in high while the second went low, trying to take out my legs and get me on the floor. I knew if that happened I was probably dead, so I did a duck, dodge, weave thing and managed to stay out of the vamps' reach. The second one got a little too close, and I swiped at him with my blade, cutting a long furrow down his arm. He snatched back his arm with a hiss.

"That's what you get for messing with a Hunter."

He wasn't amused. He snarled and came at me again at the same time the other vamp made another play for my leg. I kicked him in the face and followed up with a fireball at vamp number two. The fire ball missed. My foot didn't.

Vamp Number One flew backward, blood spurting from his nose while Vamp Number Two rushed me again and got a blade across his chest for his trouble.

I tried to throw another fireball, but the thing sort of fizzled. Was I running out of energy? Could Fire do that? I had no idea. I'd never tried throwing multiple fireballs before. In fact, the only time I'd thrown a fireball before was by accident.

Vamp Number One was back, fangs bared. He grabbed my left arm, ignoring the serious damage the Fire was doing to his hand, and flung me across the room and into Number Two's arms. A sinewy arm locked around my throat and squeezed. I struggled to draw in air but I was out of luck. Time to stop playing.

Grabbing his arm with my left hand, I waited for the fire to burn him. Only it didn't. Apparently I was completely out of juice. Shit. So, I stabbed him in the thigh with my blade. I must have hit the femoral artery because blood sprayed everywhere. The vamp howled, his arm loosening enough for me to draw in a breath.

I reached down for the Fire again, but what came out was something completely different, something I'd never seen before. A surge of something icy and blue spilled from my metaphorical center out through every pore, mixing with whatever was left of the Fire. For a split second, I was blind, deaf, dumb. There was nothing but me and the swirling, frigid blue.

My vision cleared, and I realized the entire dome was filled with swirling clouds of white. I winced as it touched my skin, leaving a small red mark. Steam. What the hell?

Shrieks reached my ears as the vamps were engulfed in clouds of steam. I couldn't see what was happening, but clearly it was causing them tremendous pain. I stepped

91

back, touching the stones of the wall behind me. They were slick and strangely cold despite the heat of the steam.

I listened carefully to the retreating footsteps of the vampires. They were escaping through the tunnel. Clearly the steam was causing them enough pain they were willing to risk sunlight to get away from it. I'd never heard of steam being used as a weapon against vampires. Perhaps it should be explored further. I made a mental note to mention it to Tessalah.

The steam began to clear, sinking toward the floor. The air turned chilly. How odd. Then I heard something. Haakon. He was shouting, but I couldn't make out the word. And then it came to me.

"Run!"

# # #

I stared at him dumbly for a moment before realizing the vamps weren't the only ones headed for the tunnel. Haakon was moving like the hounds of hell were on his heels. What on earth? I glanced around, trying to figure out what was going on. And then I saw it.

As the steam sank to the floor, it cooled and turned liquid, spreading pools of water across the floor. Up from the earth bubbled tiny springs which grew bigger by the moment. The walls were dripping with water. No, make that streaming with it. Water gushed around the fitted stones and through the narrow cracks. There was already a couple of inches of water on the floor, and even as I watched, it climbed higher. One of the burbles suddenly burst into a geyser, followed by another and another. Plumes of water burst through the floor, shooting to the ceiling. I was already drenched to the skin, as wet as I'd been when I climbed out of the ocean. The water was to my ankles now and climbing fast.

"Move it," Haakon shouted. His hair had turned dark with wet, plastered to his head.

"What the hell?"

"No fucking clue, but unless you want to drown, you better move your sweet ass."

I moved, ducking through the tunnel, I sort of crab-walked as fast as I could. By the time I was halfway through, Haakon close behind me, the tunnel was already half-filled with water. The vamps were nowhere in sight. I was starting to worry we wouldn't make it out in time.

I saw daylight ahead. We were close. By now the water was up to my chin, and panic was making my heart pound. I'd have probably been sweating if I wasn't nearly submerged. My movements were awkward against the slippery mud and rocks. A chunk of wet earth fell out of the side of the tunnel and plopped into the rising water. The tunnel was collapsing. I crawled faster.

I was inches from the exit when a sudden gush of water swept through the tunnel, filling it to the top. I barely had time to hold my breath before I was completely underwater. Gathering every ounce of will I had left, I forced down the rising panic and rushed forward, bursting up and out through the trapdoor opening. I drew in deep lungsful of air, gasping and sputtering. I hauled myself out of the tunnel as quickly as I could, knowing Haakon was behind me, still underwater.

93

I heaved myself onto dry ground and lay gasping for breath next to the little pool which had formed inside the shed. Outside the sun was climbing in the sky, the light taking on a faint greenish tinge as it filtered through the lush leaves. Where had the vampires gone? Had they stepped outside and immolated? They must have. I didn't see them anywhere.

The water surged, and Haakon popped to the surface. He, too, hauled himself out of the water and sat, legs still dangling in the pool, gasping for breath.

"What happened?" I asked again.

He shook his head, drops of water spraying around him. "One minute we were fighting the damn vamps, next there was steam everywhere. It was burning them, so they ran. And then... water."

"Maybe we triggered a booby trap?" I suggested lamely. I knew better. I'd caused the steam. And the water. I just didn't want Haakon knowing about it quite yet.

He frowned. "Maybe. Where'd they go?"

"Outside, I'm guessing. They should have burned, but I don't see any dust."

He staggered to his feet and out the door. "No. No remains. They didn't dust. They were pretty old vamps. My guess is there was enough cover they made it into the denser forest before they burned."

"Damn." I hauled myself slowly to my feet and joined him outside. "That is not what I wanted to hear."

"Not to worry. I can track them." My face must have reflected my misgiving. He shot me a scowl. "You doubt me?"

"Um, well, not *doubt* exactly..."

94

He grunted, turning his back on me to scan the trees around the shed. He carefully walked the perimeter of the small clearing, searching for tracks or something.

"Where's Kabita?" She hadn't been with him when we joined up, and she must be worrying by now.

"I didn't see her in town. She's probably still back at the rendezvous point."

And freaking the hell out, no doubt. "I think I'd better get her. We're going to need her if we're going to tromp through the jungle after those things."

He shrugged, clearly still focused on his self-appointed task. I shook my head. Men.

# # #

Finding my way back to town was marginally easier than finding the shed had been. I found Kabita lounging at a tiny round table outside the cafe/bar, sipping a drink and catching some rays. One silky black brow rose at my approach, but she said nothing. Just took another sip from her white mug and let out a long sigh.

"They really have excellent coffee here." She looked completely at home, but I noticed her eyes never stopped scanning the street. Watching. Waiting. She may have seemed relaxed. She was anything but.

"Uh, yeah, sure," I said, wishing I had the time to sit down and enjoy a cup. I was running on fumes. "We found the vamp. Sort of."

She glanced at me over the rim of her mug. "Sort of?"

"Well, turns out there was a nest." I gave her a quick rundown of what had happened, up to and including the flooded tunnel and the nest escaping into the jungle.

She let out another long sigh when I'd finished. "Why me?"

"Excuse me?"

"Never mind." She took a long last swallow of coffee, threw a few bills down on the table—I had no idea how she'd kept them dry—and strode down the street in the direction I'd come from like an avenging goddess. "Let's go dust these assholes."

I raised both eyebrows at that. Kabita never swore. Well, almost never. It had to be pretty serious if she was pulling out the potty mouth.

"Haakon is trying to pick up their trail." I was pretty sure she could hear the doubt in my voice. Wasn't like I was hiding it. Haakon may be a Sunwalker and a Viking—well, former Viking—but he wasn't a Hunter.

"Good." She picked up the pace with me trotting along behind her. What was with people and this fast walking crap lately?

I took the lead, showing her the way through the jungle to the clearing where Haakon waited. Except when we got there, there was no one else in sight. Just the empty shed with water still burbling out the open door.

"Where's Haakon?"

I gave an irritated growl. "I told him to wait here for us. Jackass probably decided to go all manly and follow the vamps on his own. Idiot." I ignored the fact I'd virtually done the same thing myself. I strode around the edge of the clearing, looking for the spot where Haakon had entered the jungle. Sure enough, he'd practically left a giant, flashing neon sign for us to follow. Apparently Vikings had never learned the fine art of blending in. I shushed the inner voice that told me he'd deliberately made the way obvious so we could follow. "This way."

Haakon had left a wide swath through the jungle. Broken branches and vines, bruised leaves, and trampled underbrush clearly marked the way. I really hoped he'd done it on purpose. Otherwise he was just about the klutziest person I'd ever met.

A giant spider web hung suspended between two large palm trees, its occupant glaring at me. I really am not fond of spiders, so I skirted it as quickly as I could. A low-hanging vine slapped me in the face, its lush green leaves glossy in the dappled sunlight. I batted it away. All around was a profusion of wild color from pink, yellow, and peach hibiscus to the purples and reds of wild orchids. A bird called somewhere in the distance, and I could have sworn I heard the chatter of monkeys.

Kabita and I must have gone about two miles before we caught up with Haakon. The sun was high overhead, and breathing the jungle air was like inhaling soup, heavy and thick and way too hot. My body was screaming for a bottle of cold water.

He was crouched behind a clump of bushes. He waved us over, placing his forefinger on his lips. So now he wanted quiet? We scurried over and crouched beside him.

"What the hell?" I hissed. "I told you to wait for me."

"And I found the direction of our quarry. I knew you'd be able to follow."

"Uh, yeah. You left a freaking highway out there. A blind man could have followed."

He gave me an exasperated look. "Not me. The vampires. They were more worried about getting caught in the sun than being subtle."

"No shit."

"Why are we here?" Kabita interrupted our spat.

"Take a look." Haakon nodded in the general direction of the bushes.

After exchanging a glance, Kabita and I craned our necks to see around the shrubbery. We were at the edge of the jungle. Below us sprawled a small town built along the hillside, staggered so nearly every house had a magnificent view of the blue waters of the bay below. Beyond the bay, the ocean sparkled in the midday sun. Someone nearby was barbecuing. The scent of charcoal smoke and roasting meat made my mouth water and my stomach grumble. I hadn't eaten in a while.

"Okay," I said, sinking down next to Haakon. "The vamps headed here. But they couldn't have left the shelter of the trees. Not without dusting."

"Unless someone was waiting for them."

Shit. That wouldn't be good. An entire nest of vamps taking up residence in a town this size spelled nothing but trouble. I took another peek down the hill.

"All right, let's assume someone did meet them. Brought blankets or something. They still couldn't have gone far. For one thing they wouldn't have lasted long in full sun, even wrapped in blankets. For another, they would have been seen. A town this size, the gossip would be all over the place in minutes. I don't think whoever is hiding the nest would want that."

"Agreed," Haakon said. "That's why I'm thinking that house." He pointed to a pastel pink structure close to where we were hiding. It was only a short walk downhill. Someone moving fast could cover it in seconds.

"Makes sense," Kabita agreed. "It's the only one with a door on this side."

She was right. The wooden door had been painted pink to match the rest of the house, but anyone could clearly see there was a door. "A neighbor could still have seen something. There are plenty of windows facing this way."

"Yeah, but most people will be at work this time of day," Kabita pointed out. "And tourists will be down at the beach. If they moved fast, nobody would notice."

It made sense. But there was one way to know for sure. "You two stay here. I'll go check."

"Morgan..." Haakon started to say, but I ignored him.

I slipped from our hiding place and strode toward the pink house. I walked tall and easy, striding along as if I had every right to be there. I'd learned that, generally speaking, if you acted like you had a right to be in a place, everyone else assumed you did. Of course, that didn't work with vampires, but I was more concerned with neighbors than denizens of the night.

I walked straight up to the pink door and pretended to knock. Anyone watching would assume I was an ordinary visitor. I took a deep breath and waited for my spidey senses to kick in. Sure enough, there was that gripping tingle at the back of my skull. There were vamps inside.

Chapter Eleven

"We should wait until full dark." Kabita shot a scowl at the pink door. "Less likely to be spotted by neighbors."

"And more likely to have escaped vamps on our hands." I shot her down. "Nope. We need to get in there now."

"And how do you suggest doing that? It's a thick door. Pretty sure people will notice a giant Viking kicking it down." Kabita refused to give up.

"I've got other ways," I said.

"Oh, right. Miss Fire Happy. Let's burn the door down. It's not like anyone will see and call the fire department."

I sighed. "They might. But it'll give us time to get in there and hopefully dust the nest before anyone arrives to check out the fire." If my Fire was even working again.

"Because that's worked so well for us in the past."

We stood there glaring at each other, arms crossed like a couple of kids. This was getting us nowhere.

"Fine," I said. "We need a diversion. Something that will get the neighbors out of their houses and paying attention to something else."

"That makes sense," Kabita agreed. "Got any ideas?"

"Not exactly," I admitted.

"I've got an idea," Haakon said.

We both stared at him. "What?"

"Better I show you." He stood up and whipped off his shirt, revealing acres and acres of taut, rippling muscles covered in golden brown skin. Kabita and I sucked in our breath. Good gods, he was a fine specimen of manhood. His

100

hands went to his jeans zipper. Down it came and off went the jeans, leaving Haakon standing there in nothing but a pair of indecently snug heather-gray boxer briefs and scuffed black combat boots. I closed my eyes, reminding myself I had a boyfriend I loved like crazy.

"This plan involves you getting naked?" Kabita finally choked out. I opened my eyes. She was staring at him like she wanted to eat him alive. Couldn't say I blamed her.

"Indeed." He shot us a wide, white smile. "Be ready." And with that he strolled out from behind the bush and down the hill like he owned the place.

"Sweet baby Jesus," Kabita breathed.

"You're not kidding."

Haakon sauntered casually between the pink house and its blue neighbor. As he moved out onto the street, he began to stagger and weave like a drunk. Then in a thick Norwegian accent he began belting out, "My baby takes the morning train."

"Oh good lord," I gasped. "The man can't hold a tune in a bucket."

"You got that right." Kabita was barely holding back a laugh as doors and windows opened and people began appearing on the street, pointing and laughing at the nearly naked "drunk" tourist. "Guess that's our cue. My bet is we're going to have to stage a jail break after this. You ready?"

"As I'll ever be."

It was my turn to stride down the hill toward the pink house, Kabita close on my heels. I laid my palm flat on the sun-warmed wood and reached down inside me for the Fire. I guess it had recovered, because it came in a rush, spreading down my arm and onto my hand. I concentrated on pouring the fire into the wood. Within seconds the door began smoking and charring, and then the Fire caught. Kabita and I stepped back and watched as the door began to burn in earnest. We still heard Haakon belting out songs down the street, a show tune this time.

"That boy had better not quit his day job," Kabita muttered. "Unless he plans to take up stripping."

I snorted. "Okay, ready?" The fire was beginning to sputter, and the door was thoroughly charred, even burned through in some places.

"As I'll ever be," Kabita echoed my words.

One swift kick, and the door crumbled into so much ash and rubble. Kabita and I stepped inside.

# # #

Light spilled through the open doorway, lighting up a narrow vestibule with a white tiled floor and a narrow staircase leading to the floor above. On the left side of the hall directly across from us were closed doors. Somebody had taken the time to weather-strip the crap out of them. Definitely a good place for a bunch of vamps to hang out.

"This is definitely it."

Kabita nodded and stepped to the left. Twisting the doorknob, she shoved the door open and shone her flashlight into the kitchen beyond.

"Where's yours?" she asked.

"Didn't bring one."

She shot me a look. "You didn't?"

I shrugged. I didn't bother pointing out I could see better in the dark without one. I didn't like reminding her I was a freak and getting freakier by the second. Not in a good way, either, if that whole flooding thing was anything to go by. Yeah, I was pretty sure that had been me, but I really didn't want to think about it right now.

Since Kabita was going left, I went straight to the second closed door. Pushing it open, I found more hallway and closed doors. Fantastic.

Straight ahead was the front door. All the glass inserts had been covered over with tin foil and duct tape, and weather-stripping had been tacked around the cracks to prevent even the tiniest amount of light from seeping through. There was a door on either side of the hall. Same deal with the weather-stripping, I guessed just in case somebody accidentally opened the front door in broad daylight. Which was doubtful, seeing as how it was barricaded with a steel bar. Nobody was opening that door from the outside.

The door to the left revealed a dining room, its giant picture window covered in more tin foil and topped by a heavy velvet curtain. Totally out of place in the tropics. I could make out a long table large enough to seat twelve. Matching chairs had been pushed back against the walls like it was a ballroom, and black garbage bags covered the floor beneath the table. Weird. Another door led to what I assumed was the kitchen. I left the room to Kabita and crossed to the other side of the hall.

The main room ran the full side of the house and, like the dining room, its large windows were completely blocked off. Still, I could easily make out the low huddled forms of sofas, easy chairs, and side tables. The room was as empty as the rest of the house, but still I could feel that gripping on the back of my skull that told me vamps were nearby.

"I'm headed upstairs." Kabita's whisper broke the silence. I turned to see her standing in the doorway, her flashlight pointed at the floor so it wouldn't blind me. Who was I kidding? Kabita knew all my best freakish qualities.

"Sure thing. I'm going to poke around down here some more." I couldn't say why, but I had the strongest feeling our answers lay here, not on the floor above. Kabita nodded and disappeared. I could just make out the sound of her footsteps ascending the back stairs.

I returned to prowling the room. Heavy velvet drapes graced every window despite the aluminum foil. Double security, I guessed. Someone had hung matching drapes on the opposite wall to balance the room. It was weird, but it kind of worked. All dramatic and stuff. I frowned, wondering why. The room wasn't *that* large that it needed balancing. Why not just paint the wall or hang pictures or something? Why hang curtains?

I swished back the first curtain, revealing bare white wall. The next was the same. By the time I reached the last curtain, I was starting to think I was an idiot, but instead of bare wall, there was a cheap wooden door.

"Oh, bravo," I murmured, pushing it open. A set of stairs led down into what was clearly a basement. All righty then.

Leaving the door open, I made my way around the room, shoving back curtains and ripping foil off the windows. Light flooded the space and filtered down the stairs. Perfect. Anyone running up here would either be human, or they'd dust. Well, they could be demon, but hopefully it wouldn't come to that.

Blinking my eyes against the bright light, I made my way quietly down the stairs. My eyes quickly adjusted to the dim light, sharpening edges and picking out details. I cursed silently as I realized the Darkness had risen again without my bidding. We were going to have a chat one of these days, the Darkness and me.

At the bottom of the stairs was yet another door. What was with these people and doors? I pushed it open to reveal another hallway with still more doors. The door on the left was a small storage room filled with random bits and pieces: old cans of paint, the remains of a broken chandelier, a box of faded, dusty magazines. Nothing to get excited about. The door on the right.... I pushed it open and immediately froze. I could hardly comprehend what I was seeing.

It was a small room, maybe eight feet by eight, with a low ceiling and fake wood paneling. The red shag carpet under my feet had seen better days, and the brass sconces on the wall held fake electric candles. It was like something out of a really bad '70s porno, complete with the large, faux mahogany desk in the middle of the room. And behind that desk? Alister Jones.

"Morgan," he said, placing the tips of his fingers together in a classic Evil Villain move. He actually looked pleased to see me.

"Alister," I spat, "what are you doing here?"

"Oh, a little of this. A little of that." He tapped his forefinger on something lying on his desk. I craned my neck to see. It was a book. I recognized the symbol on the cover.

It was the book Jack and I had been all over half of France looking for.

I scowled at him. "That book does not belong to you." I had to get it away from him. We still had no idea what we needed it for, only that leaving it in Alister's hands was a really bad idea.

He ignored me. "I've been waiting for you."

"Excuse me?"

His smile was beyond smarmy and into the creepy zone. Then he frowned. "Your amulet."

"What about it?" Great. Now Alister was obsessed with the thing.

"You're not wearing it." His eyes narrowed, anger flashing in their depths.

"No. I'm not." And that was all he was getting from me. I could almost see the frustration boiling beneath his skin. I had no idea what Alister had planned for me and my amulet, but leaving it behind on the ship had been an unexpected stroke of brilliance. Curses. Foiled again, eh, Alister?

"Ah well, no matter," he said, picking up a silver letter opener and twirling it between his fingers before placing it back on the desk. "I have a lovely little surprise for you. Oh, and by the way? You'll never get your hands on this book."

Before I could open my mouth, the room was plunged into darkness. I heard rushing sounds and the grip on the back of my skull screwed down so tight, I thought my head might explode. I was surrounded by vampires.

Chapter Twelve

I didn't have time to let my eyes adjust. It was so deeply black, I couldn't see a thing though I knew they could see me just fine. I heard them, though. Sensed them. The dagger was in my right hand, wrist blade in my left.

I knew it was cheesy, but I couldn't help myself. "Let's dance, boys."

I slashed with my left hand first, knowing they wouldn't expect it. Steel connected with flesh. and cool, thick blood spilled over my hand and arm. I slashed right next, slicing someone up good if the cry of pain was anything to go by. I kicked straight ahead and connected with something solid. I heard a crack and a howl. Thrust an elbow back, slash, kick, repeat.

It was too much. There were too many of them. The Darkness rose, lending strength and speed to my movements, turning the pitch black into dim gray. Still, it wasn't enough. Where was Kabita?

My dagger slipped from my hand and clattered to the floor, blood turning my skin so slick, I couldn't keep a grip on it. One of the vamps grinned wickedly, flashing fang. He rushed me on the right side, knowing I was now vulnerable.

The two of us crashed into the desk, my hip hitting the edge so hard I knew it was going to leave an amazing bruise. With the vamp's hand in a vice around my left wrist, and my blade lying useless on the floor, I was out of weapons. Then I remembered the glint of silver between Alister's fingers. The letter opener!

I reached out with my right hand, patting around on the desktop until I felt the letter opener beneath my palm. I wrapped my fingers around the handle, gripping the tiny blade tightly. With all my strength, I thrust upward, burying the knife in the side of the vamp's neck. His eyes widened as I yanked the blade back out, dark blood oozing in thick rivulets from the wound. With a roar, the vamp backhanded me so hard I saw stars.

Something broke loose inside me. I want to say it was rage, but it was more than that. It rose, ice cold and deadly calm.

I. Would. Finish. This.

I'm not sure what I thought I was doing. With the Darkness riding me, I felt no fear. I brought up my knee, hard. Instinctively, the vamp doubled over despite the fact vampires don't feel much in the way of pain. The minute he did so, my knee came up again, smashing him in the face. I lashed out with my foot, kicking him in the head so hard he tumbled across the floor before jumping to his feet with a snarl. As the vamp rushed me, I simply raised my left hand, palm facing him. The new thing flooded my veins, a rush of icy liquid, chilling me to the bone. It swirled up and through me, down my arms to my fingertips, pooling in the center of my palm. I took a deep breath and then....

As I thrust out my hand, something flew from the center of my palm and lodged itself in the vampire's heart. The creature stared down at the thing sticking out of its chest, then back up at me, eyes wide. It opened its mouth and burst into a cloud of dust. The thing I'd thrown at the vamp hit the floor with a dull *thud* and shattered into a million pieces that bounced across the carpet like tiny, shimmering diamonds.

"Sweet gods above," I whispered, hardly believing my own eyes. I'd just killed a vamp with a freaking icicle. That wasn't normal.

There were still half a dozen more vamps to worry about. I had no time to think on what was normal or why I could suddenly throw shards of ice. This new power came surprisingly easy. I shoved the bloody letter opener in my jeans pocket in case I needed it later. Then, using both hands, I threw another icicle, and another. Within seconds I'd downed another three vamps. But with each icicle, I was growing colder, my movements slower. My entire body was starting to feel numb. Something from a long ago survival class niggled at my brain. Hypothermia. This new power of mine might be awesome, but it came with one hell of a nasty side effect.

I stopped throwing icicles and dug into my pocket with numb fingers for Alister's letter opener. The vamp blood had turned sticky on the handle, and my icy cold skin stuck like a tongue stuck to a frozen lamppost.

I knew the letter opener wasn't much of a weapon, so I made a dash across the room before the vamps were on me. Leaning down, I scooped up my blade. This one didn't stick so badly. Thank the gods for leather handles.

As I continued slashing and hacking and kicking, I tried to force the ice back down to that place inside me where my powers lived. To no avail. I was too sluggish and weak. Even the vamps could see it.

I did the only thing I could think of. I called Fire.

It ripped through me so fast, it left me gasping for breath. Fire shot from my fingers in hungry streamers, licking at the skin of the vamps, blackening it. They screamed in pain, rushing away from me, toward the stairs and daylight. I ran after them, the carpet squishing under my boots. The Fire had melted the ice. I no longer felt cold, but flushed and feverish. The Fire was out of control, licking at the walls, the ceiling. This house was going to turn into an inferno with Kabita and me still inside.

As the Fire lit up the blackness of the basement, I saw that Alister was gone. Damn him.

Screams erupted from the stairwell. The vamps had made it to the top of the stairs before realizing, too late, that bright sunlight spilled through the now open windows, bathing the living room above in deadly rays. The first one burst into dust before the rest hustled back downstairs only to be greeted by the Fire. And me.

I strode slowly toward them, dagger in one hand and letter opener in the other, ignoring the exhaustion that pulled at my limbs. I must have looked freaky as hell, because they appeared to be scared to death, their glowing red eyes fixed on my face. Except vampires were rarely scared, not like this. Their terror was almost palpable.

It hit me. Souls. Every single one of them had souls. Fuck Alister and his damn technology.

"I release you."

The words weren't mine, though I'd spoken them before. They came from the Darkness. Or maybe from something else, who knows? But they came out of my mouth as the Fire licked up the walls toward the trapped vampires.

I watched as the Flame and the sun took them. Ashes to ashes. Dust to dust. As their remains drifted slowly down through the air, I walked calmly up the stairs and out into daylight. Behind me, the fire raged out of control.

# # #

I didn't remember making it outside, but I must have, because the next thing I knew, I was laying on my back in the grass, staring up at the impossibly blue sky. I coughed a little, my throat tickled by smoke, but other than that, I felt fine. A little overly warm maybe, but that could have been due to being in the tropics.

"Morgan. Oh my goddess, Morgan, say something."

I blinked as Kabita's face came into view, hovering over me. "Oh, good," I mumbled. "You made it out."

"Of course I did," she hissed. "Now stop this before the neighbors see."

"Can't stop a house fire." The very idea was absurd. And was that a rock poking me between the shoulder blades? How rude.

"Not that, you ninny. The *Fire*. You're still channeling it."

Oh, shit. I hadn't realized. The Fire had always been the hardest of my powers to control. The wild nature of it, I supposed. I tried to pull it back down into its hole, but it refused. It was out, and it liked being out. It wanted to burn. Burn everything.

Water was Fire's natural enemy, but calling it was out of the question. I'd nearly frozen myself to death with it. Earth. Yes. Dirt put out a fire, right? That's what people who camped did. Threw dirt over the fire pit to put it out. Not that I knew about such things personally, as I found camping a ridiculous pastime. Still, if throwing dirt was needed, I could do that.

I reached down into my metaphorical core and called for Earth. It came slowly, no hurry, easing its way through me, unfurling gently like a blossom or a vine. It twined its way through my body, creating that green shimmer only I— and possibly a few magical others—could see. Mentally I sent it toward the burning building. I saw it twisting and curling its way over the grass and up the sides of the house, across the roof, through the windows, down the chimney. Wherever it touched, the Fire retreated. Sulkily, like a child who has had its favorite toy taken away.

I called the Earth back to me, and it came, calmly, as if to thumb its nose at the unruly Fire. The Fire slunk back with it, firmly put in its place. I grabbed them both, the Earth gently, but the Fire with a very firm grip, and pulled them back inside myself. Then I slammed the metaphorical lid on them both and lay back on the grass with a sigh. I was bone-deep exhausted. All I wanted was a nap.

"You okay?" Haakon's face appeared beside Kabita's.

"Yeah, fine." I wasn't fine, but I didn't want to look like a wuss. Besides, what could he do about it?

"Find anything?"

Kabita shook her head. "No tech. I think Morgan found some vamps."

Haakon raised an eyebrow. Why could everyone do that but me?

"Yeah," I said, slowly sitting up, realizing I was still gripping blades in either hand. My mouth tasted like week-old socks, and a headache pressed behind my eyes. "They're dust."

"Good. I don't suppose you found who was controlling them," he said.

"Oh, I didn't say that," I said, sliding my dagger into my boot before heaving myself to my feet. I ignored his offered hand. I might be a bit wobbly, but I wasn't an invalid. The minute I was standing, or rather swaying, I shoved the bloody letter opener into my pocket. No sense disturbing the neighbors any more than they already were.

Kabita's eyes widened. "You saw who it was?"

"Better. We had a nice little *tête-à-tête*."

She narrowed her eyes. "Oh, really. Do tell."

"It was your father, Kabita. It was Alister Jones. He's got the book. And we need to go after him before he finds a way off this island."

# # #

We left the burning house behind us. The neighbors were too busy gawking at the blaze to worry about three random tourists. They had even forgotten Haakon's bizarre behavior in the wake of this new excitement. I heard the wail of a fire engine in the distance. The three of us picked up our pace, trotting downhill toward the center of town and the harbor.

"Are you sure it was my... I mean Alister?" Kabita asked. A frown marred her usually placid face. It took a lot to rattle Kabita.

"Definitely. No doubt about it. He even taunted me about the, uh...about stuff." I didn't want Haakon knowing

113

too much about the book. He might be a Sunwalker, but he was an unknown factor in this...whatever this was. War, maybe?

Haakon shot us a glance. "You saw Alister Jones? Here? On the island?"

"Yeah. And we need to get a move on. He's way ahead of us." We picked up the pace, moving almost at a jog. I turned to Kabita. "He left this behind. Thought maybe you would want it." I pulled out the letter opener.

She stared at it in distaste. "Vampire blood?"

I gave a slight shrug. "I needed a weapon. It was handy."

"No, thanks," she said. "I don't want anything of that man's."

I couldn't say I blamed her. Since I was low on weaponry, I tucked the letter opener away. Never knew when something like that would come in handy. "You find anything in the house?"

"No sign of the soul vamp tech anywhere and nothing that would point us to where it is. You?"

I shook my head. "No tech downstairs, either. Just Alister and a whole lot of vamps."

"He wouldn't have it here," Haakon said, falling into step beside us.

"Excuse me?" We both turned to stare at Haakon.

"This soul vamp technology you keep talking about. Jones wouldn't have brought it here. He would keep it in a safe place." He said it slowly as if he was talking to a couple of idiots.

"But then how could he create soul vamps?" I asked archly. "He's got to have the tech to do that."

"Sure. But he probably turned these on the mainland and brought them here. It's not that far. He could easily fly them over at night or bring them in the cargo hold of a ship. Like the ones on-board my cruise ship."

"Okay, good point," I agreed. "But why?"

"That," Haakon said grimly as we arrived at the marina, "is the question."

While Hakkon and Kabita made inquiries at the marina, I hot-footed it to the largest, snazziest hotel on the bay. It was the sort of place that catered to the "discerning traveler." In other words, rich people. Everything was immaculate and fresh, and the employees wore perfectly pressed uniforms. Giant urns filled with tropical flowers perfumed the lobby, but underneath I could smell barbeque wafting over from somewhere nearby. My stomach gave an unladylike rumble, reminding me I hadn't eaten in far too long.

The desk clerk gave me a startled look. I'd swum through the ocean, tromped through the jungle, been flooded out of a dirt tunnel, and fought a bunch of vampires. Oh, and I'd lit a house on fire. I must have looked a sight.

He cleared his throat, straightened his shoulders, and gave me a wide, professional smile. "How may I help you?" His tone was carefully neutral.

"Is there an airport on this island?"

His eyes widened. "Of course not, Madame. The island is too small for a runway."

"Then how do people get here other than by boat?"

"Sometimes a float plane lands in the harbor. Occasionally guests arrive by helicopter." His tone was calm, unflappable, but I could see it was a struggle. He was trying hard not to stare at my singed clothing or the dirty footprints I'd left on the white marble floor.

"Okay, let's say they want to leave. Where would they grab one of these helicopters?"

He licked his lips. "Well, Madame, they would either need to have their own helicopter, or they'd need to hire one. In either case, there is only one place a helicopter can safely put down."

"And that is?"

"The helipad just outside town."

"Where exactly?"

He pulled a glossy trifold brochure from beneath the counter, unfolded it, and laid it flat on the counter. There was a small map of the island with various points of interest marked with large black dots. "We are here." He drew a big X over the spot on the map where the hotel was. "The helipad is here." He drew another mark about a mile or so out of town. "The only way to get there is by taxi. Or walking."

"How about a phone number?"

"Certainly, Madame."

I was getting heartily sick of him calling me "Madame," but at least we were getting somewhere, so I held my tongue. He tapped a few keys on his computer, then scrawled a number on the map. "This is the phone number. If anyone is in the office. They don't keep regular hours."

"Thanks," I said, grabbing the map. "How about a phone?"

He pointed across the lobby to a cream-colored phone fixed to the wall. "There is a customer courtesy phone. Feel free."

"Thanks again." I strode across the lobby and quickly dialed the number. Somebody answered on the sixth ring.

"'Lo."

"Is this the helipad?"

"Sure."

"Have you had any helicopters fly in or out in the last couple hours?"

"Sure."

This was going nowhere. "Did a man named Alister Jones fly out today?"

"Dunno."

I wanted to scream into the phone. Instead I told myself to enhance my inner calm and tried again. "Did a helicopter carrying male passengers fly out within the last couple hours?"

"Sure."

Now we were getting somewhere. I quickly described Alister Jones, down to his pink and blue striped shirt. "Was he the passenger that flew out?"

"Yup."

"Fantastic. Do you know where they were headed?"

"Nope."

"How about which direction they flew?"

I could almost hear him shrug. "West? But that don't mean nuthin'."

He was right, of course. Whatever direction the helicopter had flown initially, they could easily change course once they were over open water. Did helicopters even need to file flight plans? I was pretty sure they didn't, which sort of left us up a creek.

"Thanks for your time," I mumbled before hanging up.

Alister Jones could be anywhere by now. We'd lost him.

Chapter Thirteen

We had no choice but to return to the ship. There was nowhere else to go. Nowhere else to look. The nest was destroyed, Alister gone, and the people on the islands safe, at least from those particular monsters. Other sorts of monsters weren't really my forte.

Once aboard, Haakon gave us a brief, stilted goodbye before returning to his duties. Kabita and I met up with Eddie to get my amulet back and give him a rundown of everything that had happened, including my run-in with Alister.

"Alister gets wilier by the moment," Eddie grumped. "No offence intended." He patted Kabita's hand.

"None taken."

"Ladies, I want to thank you both for coming to my rescue. I don't know what we would have done without you." He gave the hem of his mustard yellow waistcoat a tug.

I grinned. "No problem, Eddie. Just consider us your knights in shining armor."

He laughed. "I'll do that. Now, the cruise ends tomorrow. Any ideas about what to do next? I feel that finding Alister is becoming increasingly important and the book even more so."

I agreed with him. This whole thing had started with Alister and stopping him was the only way to end it.

"What about asking your sentient book, Eddie? Maybe it knows something about the book Alister took from France. It might even be able to tell us where he is."

He tapped his lower lip thoughtfully. "It's an idea. Of course, knowing and sharing are two different things where my sentient book is concerned. Still, I agree we should ask it."

"I'll go with you," Kabita said, turning to Eddie. "With Inigo out of commission, I've got work piled up back in Portland." She didn't say it, but I knew that me running around the planet after Alister and Inigo wasn't helping anything, either.

"How about you, Morgan?" Eddie asked. "What's your plan?"

"For now I'm headed back to the Highlands." I repressed a stab of guilt at leaving Kabita with a full plate. I needed to check on Inigo. I could only hope things had changed. If not...well, I'd cross that bridge when I got there.

Eddie and Kabita nodded. That's the thing about true friendship. Never needing to explain yourself.

# # #

By the time the plane touched down in Edinburgh, I was happy to be on solid ground again. I'd had my fill of boats, planes, Hippocampus, and dragon flight. Frankly, I wouldn't have minded spending a couple weeks lounging on that beach we'd landed on in the Bahamas. That had been one seriously beautiful stretch of sand, at least from what I could see at night, and it had been awhile since I'd had a vacation.

But I needed to be with Inigo. He might not want me there, but frankly, what he wanted didn't matter. People who loved one another stuck by each other. They didn't run away when things got hard. He needed me whether he wanted to admit it or not.

I picked up my rental car and drove north into the hills of Scotland. Several hours and a pub stop (or two) later, I was pulling into the courtyard of the dragons' keep. This time there was no one to greet me. I hadn't expected it. No one knew I was coming, after all. But I'd no doubt many eyes were on me. I could feel them boring into my back as I took the front steps two at a time. I wasn't worried, though. They didn't call me Fire Bringer for nothing.

Actually, come to think of it, I had no idea why they called me that. It was something Drago had told me the night he and Inigo met for the first time. He'd never explained and I'd chalked it up to being a dragon thing.

The hall was as deserted, as the courtyard had been. Fortunately I knew my way. A good sense of direction comes along with the whole Hunter thing.

I made my way down the hall, retracing the twists and turns I remembered from my previous visit. I was nearly to the wing where they were keeping Inigo when I heard a bellow, followed by a shout, and then something like nails scrabbling on stone. Baffled, I glanced around for the source of the odd noise.

Around the corner barreled a very small dragon. He, or maybe she, was about the size of a basset hound but covered in neon yellow scales. It took me a moment to register that the eye-shocking color wasn't natural. It was the result of what looked like an entire can of paint.

The little creature slid on the smooth marble floor, talons scrabbling against the slick stone, and skidded into me so hard it nearly knocked my legs out from under me. I managed to grab onto a nearby suit of armor. Two giant blue eyes blinked at me from beneath the still-wet paint, and I noticed I had matching streaks across the legs of my jeans. The dragon let out a bellow and then a stream of fire. The drapes behind me went up in flames, and the little dragon took off again down the hall. I stared after it with my mouth hanging open.

"Roland!"

The shout startled me, and I turned in time to see a woman dash around the corner coming from the same direction from which the dragon had appeared. She looked more than a little worse for wear. Her jeans and T-shirt were covered in soot, her eyebrows were singed, and her hair, haphazardly piled on top her head, was still smoking. A smear of neon yellow graced her right cheek.

"Have you seen Roland?" she demanded.

"Little dragon covered in paint?"

She nodded.

"He went that way." I pointed down the hall.

She frowned at the drape still burning merrily behind me. "Oh, dear."

"Don't worry. I'll get it. You go find Roland."

With a quick nod, she took off after the baby dragon, and I turned to the business of putting out a fire. I didn't see anything so ordinary as a fire extinguisher or a bucket of sand nearby. There was nothing for it. Heaving a sigh, I reached down inside me and hauled Water out of its prison. Temporary reprieve only.

I think it might have been upset with me, because while it agreeably sprayed itself all over the burning drapes, it also covered the hall in a good inch of water before icing over. The hall was now a skating rink.

"Do not make me unleash Fire again," I snapped. Drago would kill me if I messed up his castle.

With a pout, the water receded, ice and all. It slunk back into its metaphorical cave and sulked like a child. Frankly I didn't care. I was more interested in the baby dragon fiasco.

I took off running down the hall after the dragon and what I assumed was either his mother or his nanny. They weren't hard to find. I followed the bellowing and the shouting right into the library. If Roland spit fire again, there was no way I'd be able to save the books, some of them centuries old.

"Burn these books, and I will turn your hide into a new pair of boots," I shouted over both of them.

Two pair of eyes, one human and one dragon, turned to stare at me. The little dragon whimpered. The woman propped her fists on her ample hips. Roland scuttled behind her in an attempt to hide, nearly knocking her over.

"How dare you threaten this poor child."

I snorted. "Poor child, my ass. The kid's a holy terror. If he can't control himself, he doesn't belong in a library. Frankly, I don't think he belongs anywhere that isn't completely fireproof."

The woman gasped, affronted. "He's a little boy. He's just being...mischievous. He only started breathing fire a few days ago. Who do you think you are, anyway?"

I shrugged. "Nobody, really. But Drago seems to think I'm the Fire Bringer."

I wasn't prepared for the reaction. Her eyes widened in horror, and she dropped to her knees and folded her hands in supplication. "Please, Lady. Please forgive my impertinence and the child his lack of control. He is but a baby. Please forgive us, I beg you."

"Um, yeah, sure. Whatever. Would you *please* get off the floor? Geez, this is embarrassing."

The woman staggered to her feet, looking like she might be about to keel over in a dead faint. "I am truly sorry, my lady. Please..."

"Forget it. It's fine. Whatever. No harm done. Or at least not much, anyway. Drago's going to need a new pair of drapes. You're his...?"

"Nanny, my lady."

I ignored the whole "my lady" thing and knelt on the carpet. I beckoned the baby dragon. "Roland, come here."

Shyly he poked his head out from behind his nanny. I waved him over, and he slowly, timidly waddled my way. When he was close, I reached out and gave him a scratch behind the one ear that wasn't covered in paint. He gurgled in delight.

"You need to listen to your nanny, Roland, do you understand me?"

He waved his dragon head, those impossibly big eyes blinking innocently at me. Oh, he was good. I bet he had half the castle wrapped around his little talon.

"Don't play innocent with me. You've been naughty."

He bowed his head in shame, but I didn't miss the look of mischief.

"You behave, or I'll come down to your nursery and show you how a dragon behaves, got it? Or better yet"—I leaned in, eyes narrowed—"I'll send Drago."

He let out a squeal and rushed behind his nanny again. I could barely hide my grin as I stood up. "You got him now?"

"Yes, lady. Thank you, Lady."

I left her in the library with Roland, still bobbing and curtseying. I was baffled. The whole "Fire Bringer" thing meant zilch to me, but it was important to Drago, so I'd let him do his thing and officially announce me. Apparently it was a much bigger deal than I'd realized. That, or the woman had spent a little too much time chasing after recalcitrant baby dragons.

The air was thick with the sooty tang of smoke as I passed the burned curtains. An elderly man in a black suit shook his head at the damage as he took measurements and jotted them down in a small notebook. I couldn't understand the words he was muttering since he spoke in dragon tongue, but he clearly was not a happy camper.

I took the flight of stairs to the second floor and wandered down the hall toward Inigo's room. I hesitated in front of his door, suddenly wondering if I was doing the right thing making a surprise visit. Last time hadn't gone so well. I should have called. Or texted. Or emailed. Or something.

I turned and strode back down the hall toward the staircase. I should find Drago. Catch up. Let him tell Inigo I was here. Yeah. That's what I should do.

I came to a stop at the head of the stairs. Why was I being such a loser? I needed to march back down that hall, into that room, and.... And what? Demand Inigo be nice to me? Act normal? Treat me like a girlfriend he actually wanted to see instead of someone he could barely stand looking at?

As I waffled, my cell phone rang. I breathed a sigh of relief as I pulled it out of my pocket. I'd been given a temporary stay. I frowned as I read the screen. Jack.

"Why the hell haven't you called me?" I snarled into the phone. So much for phone etiquette.

"Hello to you, too," he snapped.

"What the hell, Jack? You take off, leave me alone in Paris without so much as a word. You don't return my calls or texts. Nobody knows where you are."

"You're not my keeper, Morgan."

"Fuck you." Yeah, I said it. I was mad as a freaking hornet and growing angrier by the second. "You go all bullshit Guardian on me one minute, and the next, when I really need you, you fucking disappear. I think I deserve an explanation."

He let out a long-suffering sigh. It made me want to smack him.

"I didn't call to argue with you," he said. "I wanted to let you know I had a lead on the book. That's why I took off like that."

"Too late," I told him. "I already know where it is. Alister has it. He was on some island in the Caribbean, but it's too late. He escaped before we could get it." I felt smug and superior. Well, except for the Alister escaping part.

"We?"

Oh, bloody hell, here we go again. "Kabita. Me. Eddie helped." I left out the whole Haakon thing, though I really wanted to ask if Jack knew the Viking Sunwalker.

"He's okay, then? Eddie?"

"Yeah. There was a small vampire problem on his cruise ship, but everything's fine now."

"Uh-huh." I could practically see him shaking his head in exasperation. "Well, since you let Alister escape...."

"Listen, you asshat..."

"I've got a few other leads," he interrupted. "I'm going to follow them up. I'll let you know what I find."

"You do that."

"Are you back in the States?"

I hesitated. "No. I'm in Scotland."

"How is he?"

I swallowed. "I haven't seen him yet. Just got here. But I'll tell him you said 'hi.' Is that everything?" My voice was abrupt, stilted. I so did not want to talk about Inigo. Not with Jack.

Jack cleared his throat. "Yeah. That's it."

"Fine. Gotta go." I disconnected before he could say another word. The man made me want to pull my hair out sometimes. Most times. Worst Guardian ever.

Chapter Fourteen

Before I could shove my phone back in my pocket, it rang again. This time it was Kabita.

"We consulted Eddie's sentient book," she said before I could so much as say hello.

"And?"

"Nothing."

"Nothing?"

"That's what I said," she snapped. "Just gave us a big blank page. Hang on, I'm putting you on speaker. Eddie wants to talk to you."

"Morgan, you *must* get that book back as soon as possible," Eddie shouted. I winced, pulling the phone away from my ear.

"Eddie, you don't need to yell," Kabita's voice was slightly muffled, as if she'd put her hand over the mic.

"Sorry." Eddie's voice dipped to a more reasonable decibel.

"Why do I need to rush home if the book didn't show anything?" I asked.

"Because I'm hoping it will show *you* something. After all, you're the Key and it's the key to the Key."

"Don't remind me." I'd about had it with this whole Key business. It was seriously messing with my life. "Fine, I'll be home soon. In the meantime, Jack's working on some leads, so maybe he'll come up with something."

"Hang on," Kabita said. I heard a beep, and then she came back, this time with the speaker phone off. "What are your plans?"

I knew she wasn't talking about Alister or the key problem. "I-I don't know yet. I'm about to go see him." I also knew she'd realize I wasn't talking about Jack.

There was a slight pause. "Good luck." She hung up.

I had a feeling I was going to need all the luck I could get.

#

The door to Inigo's room was partially open, and I heard the murmur of voices from inside. Peering around the door frame, I saw a woman sitting on a chair next to the bed talking to Inigo. It was Tanith, my friend Cordelia's sister, and the one they called the Dragon Child. She actually had Inigo smiling. Relief flooded me. It was going to be okay.

I rapped softly on the door before stepping into the room. I grinned widely. "You're looking better."

His smile disappeared so fast that for a moment, I thought I'd imagined it. But I hadn't. He could smile for Tanith, but for me he was nothing but a cold, hard shell. My heart sank. Things weren't going to be okay after all.

"Morgan!" Tanith jumped up from her chair and flew around the bed in a swirl of bright yellow and lime green to wrap me in a hug. I had no idea what the hell she was wearing, but it was eye searing bright. "It is *so good* to see you again. How are you? You've got extra freckles. Have you been in the sun?" Her words spilled over in a bright jumble. That was Tanith for you. Where Cordelia was calm—well, calmer—Tanith was like a brightly colored super ball bouncing around like crazy, never staying still.

I touched my nose where the freckles in question had broken out. "I'm fine and yes, I have." My words were muffled seeing as how my face was half squashed against her shoulder. She smelled of lilac and lilies of the valley. It was a nice scent, but it made my nose twitch. Damn allergies. "Maybe you could let me breathe?"

She laughed as she let me go. "Oh, you have been missed."

I wasn't sure who besides her had missed me. Clearly Inigo hadn't. I cleared my throat. "How's the patient?"

Tanith started to open her mouth, but before she could say anything, Inigo snarled, "The patient is lying right here."

"Fine," I said, forcing a smile. "How are you?"

"None of your business."

"Excuse me?" I'd never wanted to slap someone so much in my life. How dare he? After all we'd been through. He was behaving worse than Jack ever had. At least Jack had been an ass because he'd been attempting to put his so-called duty first. Inigo was just plain... being an ass.

"You heard me," he growled. Then he rolled over, turning his back to me.

Before I could say something I probably would have regretted later, Tanith pulled me from the room and shut the door behind us. She sighed deeply as she led me down the hall toward the staircase. "I am so sorry," she said, keeping her voice low. Dragons had very keen hearing. "He doesn't mean it."

"Sure sounds like he does."

She closed her eyes for a moment before opening them and giving me a weak smile. "All right. He does. But not the way you think. He isn't quite himself these days."

"I thought his recovery was going well."

"It is. He's doing very well with physical therapy, but that isn't the problem."

"What is?"

She paused for a moment before slowly descending the stairs. "His mental state."

"His mental state seemed just fine a minute ago," I snapped, keeping pace beside her. "The two of you were practically having a party in there." It wasn't fair, but I couldn't help myself. Part of me was jealous. Not in a sexual sort of way—I knew Tanith and Inigo didn't have that kind of relationship—but in that sort of intimate way partners *should* have. Where they share themselves. Their thoughts. Their feelings. Inigo was sharing nothing with me. He was giving to Tanith what he should have been giving to me.

"That's because I wasn't there."

I stumbled, practically tripping down the rest of the stairs. "What do you mean?"

"Inigo has a pretty severe case of PTSD. Post-traumatic stress disorder."

"I know what it is." It came out in a snarl.

"Of course." She nodded graciously. "I'm sorry."

I was the one being an asshole, and she was being nice to me. I took a deep breath. "No, I'm sorry. I'm being a bitch, and I have no right to be. You're doing everything you can to help him. It's not your fault he...we..." I stopped. If I went any further I was going to break down and cry like a baby.

As we reached the bottom of the stairs, she stopped and took my hands in hers. "Morgan, I am so very sorry about all this. It's not your fault. Not at all. But when he looks at you, he remembers what happened and that triggers something in his mind. He starts having flashbacks, horrible nightmares. It's like he's right back there in that moment when that bloody bitch of a queen nearly ripped his heart out of his chest. Can you blame him if he can't look at you right now?"

I couldn't. Even though I wanted to. Even though it felt like it was my heart being ripped out.

"It's going to take time," she assured me. "Just give him time. Right now he's pushing you away, but eventually his mind will heal, and he'll be himself again. Able to love you again."

I gave her a smile and a nod. "Sure," I said. "You're right." But I knew she wasn't. I'd known people with PTSD before. Hunters, cops, soldiers. None of them were ever the same. Look at me. The night I died changed my life forever. People who had once been my closest friends were no longer in my life. It was just the way things were.

With a last glance up the stairs, I bid Tanith goodbye and strode out of the castle without looking behind me. If Inigo needed time, I could give that to him. It was all he would let me give.

Chapter Fifteen

I stood at the ship railing, the ocean spray peppering my face with cold drops of salty water. Above me, the wind whipped black clouds into a frenzy. As waves tossed the ship like a toy boat in a child's bathtub, rain pelted from ever darkening skies.

I knew if this storm didn't stop, the boat would go down with all hands on-board never to be seen again. Men and women screamed as they ran to and fro on the deck, terrified. There weren't enough lifeboats. Not for everyone. If this did not stop, everyone would die.

I turned to the man next to me. Surely he knew a way out of this. But what could he do, a mere human? And such a small one that. He barely came to my shoulder. His fringe of gray hair tossed about wildly in the wind and rain speckled his glasses. He looked so calm, standing there at the rail.

"Edward, you must help us," I cried, grasping for a lifeline amidst the chaos. "We will all drown." Although, what I expected him to do, I could not have said.

He simply smiled at me as though the storm raging around us was is of no consequence. Then he turned back to watch the heaving gray water below us. The howl of the wind grew louder, drowning out the passengers' screams.

"Edward" I tried again. "Please. There must be something." Though what, I did not know. What could any of us do against the mighty power of Nature herself?

"Any moment now," he said. "Patience"

With each passing second, the storm grew increasingly ferocious, and my fear grew with it. What did he plan to do? Why was he waiting? Surely he realized that time was of the essence. I reminded myself there was nothing a mere human could do, so it did not matter.

Suddenly the sea surged into the air in a great plume. Salt water sprayed in all directions, soaking me to the skin. Something emerged from the column of water. An enormous figure loomed over us: a god rising from the ocean. His skin, blue like the sea itself, gleamed wetly in the faint light of the stormy sky. His eyes glowed like the fires of Hell. He was so fierce, I quailed in terror. My legs gave out beneath me and my bowels turned to water. Surely death itself was upon us.

"Poseidon," Edward said, his voice as calm as if we were taking tea on a summer's day. "Fancy meeting you here." There was a droll tone to his voice that belied the danger we were surely in. There was steel there, too, underneath.

All I could do was stare, mouth agape, eyes darting from the massive god to the small man beside me. How could Edward stand against such a one as Poseidon? Wait a moment. Poseidon was real? I could hardly wrap my mind around such a thought. I'd seen so many things in my time, but this this topped them all.

The great god bellowed his displeasure, the heat of his breath blasting the ship. The screams of the people around us increased in volume, drowning out even the raging of the sea and the howling of the wind. Their terror was palpable. Not that I blamed them. The hair on the back of my neck was standing straight on end. And yet Edward appeared completely unaffected.

"Down boy," Edward snapped as if speaking to a yappy dog that would not behave. Much to my surprise, Poseidon obeyed, slinking down into the sea like a chastised child. As he did, the sea began to calm, the wind died down, and the clouds began to part.

I stared at Edward in surprise as a ray of sun found its way through the clouds, shining directly onto my friend. Who was he that the god of the sea obeyed him?

I woke with a start to find myself not on the prow of the ship, but still safely on a plane headed home. If one can call a tin can flying through the air at several thousand feet safe.

How fun. I had another crazy dream to add to my collection. As if there wasn't enough crazy in my life already.

What was really strange was that this time it wasn't about some dead ancient Atlantean Priest or high Priestess. It wasn't about a Fire Bearer throwing herself from a cliff. No, this was about someone I actually knew. This was about Eddie, and Eddie had bossed around Poseidon like he was a recalcitrant child. My suspicions about Eddie were growing deeper by the minute. Who exactly was he? We were going to have a talk when I got home to Portland. This time he wasn't going to blow me off.

# # #

Since time was of the essence, I went straight from the Portland International Airport to Eddie's shop, Majick and Potions. It was late in the day, but I knew he would be there. It seemed Eddie was always there when he wasn't on a steampunk cruise being attacked by vampires.

135

The parking lot was empty when I arrived, except for a lime green Vespa parked near the front steps: Eddie's preferred mode of transportation. The little bell above the door jangled as I pushed it open, and a wall of incense hit me full in the face, making my nose itch. The sneeze hit so hard, it doubled me over. Eddie really needed to open a window or something.

I wandered down the aisles, paying special attention to the gemstones as I went. A gorgeous chunk of raw aquamarine caught my eye, and I wrapped my hand around it, feeling the power flowing within. They always called to me, the gemstones. And I always reached out to them, soaking in their warmth and energy. I wasn't sure if it was one of my Powers, or if it was a Hunter thing. Or maybe I'd just lost my mind. Anything was possible.

Eddie poked his head out between the orange and gold striped curtains that blocked off the back room. "Morgan," he called cheerfully, "you made it. Tea?"

I couldn't help the smile. "Sure. Thanks." I heard rattling from the small kitchenette behind the curtain. "You and Kabita couldn't find anything out from the book, huh?"

"'Fraid not," Eddie replied, his voice muffled by the curtain. "It was most frustrating, I admit. I wish the book was more cooperative. But you know what they say about wishes and Hippocampi." There was more banging and rustling, and the sound of water filling a teapot.

"I think you mean horses, Eddie."

His head popped between the curtains again, and he frowned at me. "Do I? Are you certain?"

"Pretty sure. Yeah."

He disappeared again. "Well, that makes no sense. There are plenty of horses around. Not so many Hippocampi. In any case, we're out of luck where that book is concerned."

"Maybe it will show me something," I suggested. I doubted it, but there were other things I wanted the book to show me.

"Go ahead and try. Maybe the fickle thing will give you something it wouldn't give us."

I wandered casually behind the register and pulled out Eddie's sentient book. Laying it carefully on the counter, I glanced behind me to make sure Eddie was still busy with the tea, then I carefully flipped open the cover. I had no intention of looking for anything regarding Alister or his little book: the key to the Key, whatever that meant. At least not yet. I mean, I knew I was the "Key" in question, but what the book from France had to do with anything was a big, fat question mark. I wanted to find out what the sentient book had to say about Eddie. I felt a little bit guilty about spying on my friend, but I needed answers. Something about him wasn't adding up, and he'd been rather vague about answering questions. Not to mention that crazy dream I'd had.

As the sentient book began flipping through pages all by itself, I focused on Eddie and my dream about Poseidon. The pages finally riffled to a stop, and the book lay open to a page decorated with swirling blue and aqua waves around the edges. At the top of the page swooping gold letters spelled out "Nereus." Baffled, I quickly scanned the page. According to the book, Nereus was a figure in ancient Green mythology. He'd been a Titan, the only one who'd avoided getting sent off to where the gods had sent the Titans after the war. He was the father of the Nereids and some dude called Nerites, who looked suspiciously like a Hippocampus. He was a shape shifter with the power of prophecy, who'd aided heroes such as Hercules. He was known for his truthfulness, virtue, and passion for what was right. He was supposedly trustworthy and gentle. And as, according to Greek mythology, Poseidon was married to Nereus's granddaughter, Amphitrite, 'he was technically the grandfather-in- law of Poseidon, the god of the sea.

Holy fuckballs. Eddie was a freaking Titan? How was that even possible?

I stared at the page, the colorful words blurring before my eyes. Impossible. How could he be the grandfather-in-law of Poseidon? It was crazy, and yet I'd seen crazier. Well, maybe not crazier, but pretty darn close.

Eddie cleared his throat behind me, and I started guiltily. I turned slowly to meet his gaze. Strangely, he seemed more embarrassed than anything. A flush rode his cherubic cheeks.

"So," he said, clearing his throat. "I guess you know."

"Do I?" I glanced back down at the book. I still wasn't entirely sure I wasn't still asleep on the plane somewhere. "Is it true?"

He shrugged as he placed the tea things on the counter, rattling the teacups slightly. "I rather suppose it is."

I blinked. I took a deep breath. "That means you're one of those they called the Titans. You were here even before the gods."

"Yes, that's true," Eddie said, busying himself with the tea. "Sugar?"

I nodded, and he tossed a couple lumps of raw sugar into my teacup, followed by a splash of real cream. He swirled it around carefully before handing me the cup.

"Does it matter?" His tone was very careful.

"That you're an all-powerful being who can command the obedience of gods? That you're as ancient as the world itself, maybe even more so?" I thought about it for a moment. I couldn't seem to take it in. It was too big. Too much. It was so much easier to think of him as an eccentric man with a penchant for things Victorian. "I guess not. You're still my friend, right?"

He beamed at me, that wide grin that was full of sunshine. "Of course, Morgan. Always."

"I wish you'd told me. You know all about me. Don't you trust me?"

His smile faded, and his face fell. He looked more hang-dog than cherubic. "You are right, my dear. But I simply did not know how to tell you such a thing. How does one tell one's friend that one is..."

"Literally older than the hills?"

That startled a laugh out of him. "Indeed."

"Yeah, I guess that's a tough one." I gave him a wide grin and slammed the book shut. "Well, now I know, and all that matters is that you're my friend. You have any biscuits to go with that tea?"

Eddie snorted. "You and your British-ism's," he chuckled, handing me a plate of cookies. I could almost feel the relief radiating from him. How odd that possibly one of the most powerful creatures in the world cared what I thought of him. "Now, shall we have a look and see if the book is willing to talk about other things more important to the immediate future?"

"Sure. Let's give it a try." I bit into the tea biscuit, enjoying the sweet taste of vanilla.

I flipped open the book again. This time I focused on Alister and the key to the Key. The sentient book riffled through its pages once again, this time landing on a page covered with images in rich jewel tones. Across the top in swirly silver ink highlighted with turquoise and aqua was written the word "grimoire."

"All right," I said. "This is interesting. According to this, the key to the Key isn't just some ordinary old book. Holy crap..." I read it again to make sure. "Does that say what I think it does?"

He adjusted his spectacles and peered down at the page. "Oh, my. This says it's a relic of the Atlantean Empire."

"Atlantis?" I practically squeaked. "It's really Atlantean? Not just written in their language?"

"Not at all. It's actually from Atlantis. That isn't the most important part," Eddie said, reading further. "The Atlantean book is a sort of Book of Shadows, if you will. A grimoire of various spells and such performed by the High Priests. Though perhaps 'spells' are the wrong word seeing as how we're dealing with quantum physics here. The ancients did not refer to it as magic, as we do...."

I scanned the page quickly, noting the book was original, not a copy or translation. It was the real deal. Written by the High Priest of Atlantis himself over ten thousand years ago. A relic of the lost Atlantean empire. Holy amazeballs.

"Look," I said, tapping the page. "This says there is something in the grimoire. Spell or whatever you want to call it. Something that would allow whoever uses it to control not just vampires but any creature: humans, djinn, even the Queen of the Sidhe herself."

"Oh, Hades." Eddie had an interesting way of swearing.

"Exactly," I agreed. "Can you imagine if Alister figures out how to perform that spell?"

"All hell would break loose, quite literally."

"I don't suppose the book says where to find this grimoire?"

We both perused the page, groaning as the answer became clear. No such luck. The book said nothing about where the grimoire was located at that exact moment. Nothing about Alister or his plans. Nothing of any use at all.

"Damn." I had hoped for more.

"I couldn't have said it better myself," Eddie said, selecting a cookie from the plate. He held up the teapot. "More tea?" he asked before sloshing coppery liquid into my cup.

I thanked him and dropped in another lump of sugar. There was nothing else we could do right now, so why not have tea?

"Well, Jack is still looking for leads," I said, taking a sip of the biscuity goodness. I'm more of a coffee person, but I do love a good Assam. "Maybe he'll come up with something."

"We can only hope," Eddie said, clinking his cup against mine. "If we don't get hold of that book soon, very bad things could happen. And there will be nothing I or anyone else can do to stop them." His tone was beyond grim.

He wasn't kidding. If what we had discovered about the grimoire was correct, Alister could use it to wreak all kinds of havoc. We had to stop him before it was too late for everyone.

#

After I left Eddie's, I stopped by the office to let Kabita know I was in town, and the results of our consulting the sentient book. She was sitting behind her desk, calmly sharpening one of her many blades. She took the news of Eddie's true nature surprisingly well. But then that was Kabita for you. She took everything surprisingly well. For all I knew, she'd known who he was long before I had. She was sneaky like that.

"Have you heard from Jack?" She asked, as if that were somehow more important than the fact that one of our dear friends was an ancient Titan masquerading as an ordinary human obsessed with steampunk

"Nope," I said. "Not since Scotland. I've tried calling him a couple times, but he doesn't answer. Talk about worst Guardian ever."

That made her chuckle. "No kidding. So we've got no leads on Alister's location."

"Not a one." I paused. "Unless..."

"Yes?" She glanced up from her whetstone.

"Unless," I said. "What about Jade?"

"What about Jade?" Kabita asked, laying the stone on her desk and carefully sliding her knife back into its sheath. "You're not seriously thinking of consulting that freak are you?"

142

"Watch who you're calling a freak," I said. "She's not that different than me."

"You're kidding, right? That girl is as different from you as night from day. For one thing, she's mad as a March hare. For another she's completely homicidal."

"It's not her fault she's crazy and homicidal," I reminded her. "Darroch and the freaking Fairy Queen messed with her brain. There's no way of knowing what she would have been if they hadn't screwed things up. There's no telling what I would have been if someone had done the same to me. I lucked out. You found me first."

That was the real question. Who was the monster here? The girl who'd had magic screw with her brain? Or the one who just naturally liked to kill things? Granted it was the Darkness that enjoyed the killing, not me. But the Darkness was part of me, and that I couldn't change even if I wanted to. Did that mean I was a monster?

"You're nothing like her, Morgan." Kabita shook her head. "Anyway, what makes you think she can help? She's been locked up for months. She's had no contact with Alister. She couldn't possibly know where he is any more than I do."

Gods, it must suck to find out your father was a bigger bastard than you could have ever imagined. "Jade spent a lot of time with him at one point. Maybe she knows something, someplace he likes to go. Somewhere that's important to him. Maybe he told her about his plans. I need to try. I have to talk to her. We can't leave any stone unturned. This is far too important."

Kabita shook her head. "Fine. But don't blame me if she tries to shank you."

"Trevor will be there to protect me." I couldn't help the sarcasm.

She snorted and started shuffling through a stack of paperwork. As I left the office, I pulled my phone out of my pocket and called Trevor. If I was going to talk to Jade, I was going to need his help.

Chapter Sixteen

For the second time in as many months, I found myself bouncing over the rough terrain of the Nevada desert. The road, if it could be called that, seriously needed a new pave job, although I doubted the government would let any road workers near the place. They probably had more than enough gossip to deal with as it was without a road crew telling tales of an escaped vampire snacking on their boss. Made the alien conspiracy seem like small potatoes.

I glanced at Trevor, who was unusually stoic, hiding behind dark tinted glasses. "Thanks for this," I said. "I know you had to pull a lot of strings to get me in again."

"You have no idea." He gave me a sideways glance. "The things I do for you."

"That's what family's for. Right?"

I could almost see him rolling his eyes at me. "My life was so simple before you came along," he said, but I could hear the affection in his voice. Before I'd come along, we'd both been alone. Only children without a father. Our father was still dead, but now we had each other.

"Oh, sure, it was," I said. "Probably spent all your time down at the pub. Nothing to do, nothing to see. No demons to fight or crazy-ass sidhe to throw in jail. Poor man, your life was so dull without me."

"Don't make me drop you off in the middle of the desert."

I laughed. "I'd like to see you try."

"Don't tempt me." I could see the slightest hint of a grin curving his lips.

145

"You and whose army? No wonder they haven't given you a new partner yet."

A muscle ticked in his jaw, and I could have kicked myself. His partner had been murdered by the Fairy Queen's psycho brother. Trevor had been understandably upset and had asked me to help him find the killer. I'd always wondered if the two had been more than just work partners. But I hadn't asked. I figured if they had been, and he'd wanted me to know about it, Trevor would have told me. Since he hadn't, it was none of my damn business.

"Sorry," I muttered. "I didn't mean..."

"What's the plan?" he interrupted. He stared straight ahead, tapping his thumb on the steering wheel. Okay, subject change.

"We walk in. I ask Jade if she knows where Alister is. We get our answer. We walk out. Easy is that."

"You think it's gonna be that easy, huh?"

I shrugged. "Maybe. She seemed to be a little more forthcoming last time we saw her. I think she's finally figuring out Alister and Darroch aren't exactly on her side. Those two have been using her for their own purposes for a long time. Maybe she's finally ready to stand up for herself. Take control of her life." Jade might be a killer, but it was the three amigos who'd turned her into one. I couldn't wait to get my hands on them.

"And you think she's gonna do that by helping us?"

"We can only hope."

The car slid to a stop in front of the first checkpoint. It was a simple aluminum-sided building painted a boring cream and surrounded by a whole lot of chain-link fencing and razor wire. Trevor rolled down the window. The heat was oppressive. It hit me like a blast furnace as a face appeared at the window. I recognized the guard from my last visit. He peered into the car, face impassive as he scanned each of us carefully. "Mr. Daly. Ms. Bailey. I was told to expect you. Please proceed to the next gate." He stood back and waved us forward. It didn't make me feel very confident that he still had his gun ready.

With a small salute, Trevor continued down the gravel road. Dust kicked up behind us in a billowing cloud. All around us, as far as the eye could see, was baked earth and dusty sagebrush. This was not a place I would choose to vacation.

The second checkpoint was almost as quick and soon we were making our way down the hill to the large parking lot that surrounded Area 51. As Trevor and I climbed out of the car, it felt as if the heat and dry air were sucking the moisture from my lungs. I could almost feel my skin cracking as we approached the concrete building that housed the underground prison for the compound's more interesting inmates. I breathed a sigh of relief as we passed into the cool darkness of the entryway. I didn't even mind the pat-down from the big, burly woman who looked like she could break me in half with two fingers. I bet she could bench press a car if she had a mind to. I gave her a big smile when she was done, which she totally ignored. Instead she waved me over to join Trevor before stomping off down the hall.

We didn't have long to wait for our escort to join us. I remembered him from our first visit. The over-eager young Roberts with the wide eyes and freckled nose. He greeted us enthusiastically as he ushered us toward the bank of shiny elevators.

"Don't worry," he said. "I'm quite sure this time there won't be a jailbreak."

He was no doubt right since Brent Darroch no longer resided inside Area 51. According to Trevor, he'd been sent somewhere a whole lot worse and a whole lot more secure. Since Area 51 was about as secure as they came, I was guessing Antarctica. Served him right.

We stepped into the elevator, and Roberts pushed one of the numerous unlabeled buttons. The doors slid shut with a small ding, and the elevator began to descend much faster than I would've liked. It came to a stop with a small bounce, leaving my stomach somewhere in the vicinity of my throat. I swallowed hard, willing the bile back into place.

"Here we are," Roberts said cheerfully, ushering us from the elevator car. "We've got a room reserved for you. Don't worry, she'll be chained so she can't get to you. She's been pretty calm lately, though. Reading a lot of poetry, and meditating and stuff." He shook his head as if to say he'd seen everything.

He let us down the hall to a gray door marked with the number six in red paint. Swinging it open, he waved us inside. "The prisoner will be here any moment. Can I get you anything? Coffee? Water? Cola?"

"Thanks, Roberts. We're fine," Trevor said, giving the young man a tight smile. "We'll take it from here."

"Of course." Roberts nodded, turned to me, and gave me a gentlemanly little nod. "Ma'am. I'll be back for ya'll when you're finished." He stepped out into the hall and closed the door softly behind him. I could have sworn I heard him whistling.

We didn't have long to wait before the door opened again, and two guards strode into the room, a small figure in fluorescent orange between them. They sat Jade in the chair opposite us and locked her handcuffs to the table. Without another word they turned and strode out, shutting the door behind them.

I stared at the girl across the table. She'd changed since I last saw her. She was paler, her cheeks more gaunt, and dark roots were beginning to show in her short platinum-blonde hair. Even her posture had changed, her shoulders slightly bowed as if they carried the weight of the world. Dark circles under her eyes aged her far beyond her years.

"Hi, Jade," I said gently.

"Hey," she said, not looking at me. She stared down at the table, as if it was the most fascinating thing she'd ever seen. Her thin hands were clutched together on top of the steel table, her knuckles white.

"How are you feeling?" I asked. "I mean, are they treating you okay?"

She shrugged. "No different than before. What do you care?" Some of the old Jade arrogance returned, but only for a moment.

"I care because what was done to you was wrong. No one deserves that. No one should have to go through that, and I'm sorry you did. I want to help you. If I can. If you'll let me." Despite what she'd done to me, to Inigo, I meant every word.

She glanced up, and judging by the look on her face, she didn't believe me. She wanted to, but she couldn't. Couldn't say I blamed her. After what those bastards had done to her, I wouldn't trust anyone either.

"You been talking to a shrink?" I changed tactics.

She snorted, seeming amused. "Yeah, every damn day. Like it's going to do any good." Her very slight English accent was a little stronger today.

"Keeps the suits happy, though, doesn't it?"

She shrugged, handcuffs clinking against the table. "Yeah, I guess."

"Well, that's better than the alternative, isn't it?" I asked, and got another shrug for my trouble.

There was something I knew that Jade didn't. And that was that her shrink wasn't really a shrink. Not in the normal sense of the word. He was a supernatural, and he was the only thing standing between her and a permanent psych ward or worse. His people had the ability to manipulate brainwave patterns, at least temporarily. It was his regular suppression of the impulses put in her brain by the Queen and Brent Darroch that was keeping Jade sane. Without him, she'd still be the crazed killer I'd met months ago.

"Is there anything you need Jade? Anything I can help you with?" I asked.

She shrugged. "Get me out of here?" She glanced up, her eyes peeking through her overlong bangs. There was desperation there. I got it. Hunters 'didn't do well being locked up, and she was a Dragon Hunter. She was even less suited to confined spaces than I was.

"I wish I could," I said. "You've got a way to go before they're going to let you out of here, you know that." If they ever did. "But if you help me, it'll go a long way toward proving you're ready to rejoin society."

Her look was rife with suspicion. "How can I help you?"

"Alister Jones," I said. "Do you know where he is?"

150

"Why would I know where he is?" Her tone was defensive, but I'd seen her stiffen at the mention of his name.

"You were close once," I said. "Maybe he told you something about his plans?"

"Alister Jones left me to rot," she said bitterly. "Why would he tell me anything?"

"Okay, how about a book? A very special book. Did he ever mention that?"

She mulled that over. "Actually, he did. Yeah. He used to go on about some book he said had magical powers." She snorted. "I just thought he was crazy, you know? Or like one of those conspiracy people they always have on TV that are prepping for Doomsday or looking for aliens or whatever. I didn't think he meant an actual magical book."

"Do you remember anything he said about it or what he planned to use it for?"

She shook her head, her long bangs practically covering her face. "No. He just rattled on about how it was going to change the world. He never said anything about how or anything like that."

"He never told you where he kept it?"

"Of course not. He wouldn't tell me something like that. He did say that it was someplace obvious. Like, he always said it was so obvious no one would ever think to look there. And then he'd laugh. No, wait." Her focus grew cloudy as if she was trying to recall something. "He didn't say 'no one.' He said you."

"Excuse me?"

"Alister said the place he'd hidden the book was so obvious 'Morgan Bailey would never think to look there.'"

That didn't really help. It could be anywhere. The UK, the US. Heck, it could be anywhere in the world, knowing Alister. He could have hidden it in the Otherworld, for all I knew.

"Was there someplace he talked about going? Maybe a special place he liked to visit? A favorite vacation spot? Or somewhere he liked to go to be alone?" Trevor prompted.

Jade scrunched up her forehead as if deep in thought. "Well, there was this one place. He used to talk about wanting to go there, but I don't think he'd ever been there before. He never said why, but he was kind of obsessed with it."

Trevor and I exchanged looks. This was it. This had to be it.

"And that was?" I prodded.

"Michigan."

# # #

"Michigan? Why the hell would my father want to go to Michigan?" Despite the tinny quality of the speaker phone, Kabita clearly sounded as baffled as I felt. She was obviously shocked enough to forget herself and refer to Alister as her father. She'd been careful to avoid using that particular F word ever since she'd discovered his betrayal.

"Good question," I said. "Did he ever talk about Michigan before? Like maybe there was something there he wanted to see? A tourist trap or an historical landmark." I was trying to remember anything I'd ever heard about Michigan other than the Great Lakes.

"Not that I recall." There was a pause. "Maybe something he and your father planned?"

Once upon a time, Alister and my father, Alexander Morgan, had been friends. They'd even been partners at the SRA, the Supernatural Regulatory Agency. But then Alister had turned on my father, and, if what I'd learned so far was true, had killed him. Then he'd lied to my mother about my father's death. For years I was told nothing but lies, and then I'd met my brother, Trevor, and my father's friend, Tommy Wahenaka, and I learned things that even now I found hard to believe. But it was possible that, back when they were friends, my father and Alister had talked about Michigan. Maybe even planned something. The question was why? What was in Michigan?

"I don't know. Maybe," I said. "Anything's possible. I'll have to ask my mother. Maybe she knows something."

"Good idea," Kabita said. She changed the subject. "What time does your flight get in?"

I relayed the question to Trevor. He glanced at me, then turned his eyes back to the road. It was already dark and there were no streetlights this far out. I winced as we hit another pothole and my elbow smacked against the car door. Trevor raised his voice so Kabita could hear him on the other end of the line. "We missed the last flight out of Vegas," he said. "We'll stay the night and fly back in the morning."

"Got it," Kabita said in my ear. "Just try and stay out of trouble, okay?"

"I'll do my best."

In the dark it took us nearly four hours to get back to Las Vegas. By the time we did, I was exhausted. I felt dirty

153

and grody, and all I wanted was a hot bath and a long sleep. In that order. Oh, and some food if it wasn't too much trouble. I said good night to Trevor at the hotel room door, then called room service before stepping into the small bathroom to run a bath. The hotel had those fancy bath products in the tiny bottles, so I dumped in an entire bottle of "Tangerine Dream" bubble bath. Might as well smell good while I was at it.

Since it would be forty-five minutes before my food arrived (apparently they had to kill and pluck the chicken first), I shucked off my clothes and sank into the warm bubbly water. I leaned my head against the lip of the tub and closed my eyes. Images of the last few days flitted through my mind, but I ignored them. I needed to relax, not think about killing vampires or chasing after Alister Jones. As I relaxed I began to think about Inigo. I didn't understand what was going on with him. Oh, I knew it was the PTSD thing. If anyone understood PTSD, it was me. I'd nearly been killed by a vampire, after all. In fact, technically I *had* been killed. I still had nightmares about it. And yeah, I still hid things from the people I loved. I couldn't imagine explaining to my mother how I'd been dead. That would go over like a ton of bricks.

The point was, I'd found new people to help me through it. Kabita was one of them. Inigo was another. Was that what he was doing? Finding someone new to help him? Did he realize I understood what he was going through? That I'd been there? That I wanted to be there for him? Maybe that was the problem. Maybe he wanted to be around someone who didn't get it. Someone normal. Not like me. It was hard to pretend you were normal if you spent any time in my world.

As I lay in the bath thinking about my boyfriend—or whatever he was now—I found myself becoming increasingly morose. There's nothing like the thought that your boyfriend is slowly dumping you for something over which you had no control to make a girl feel thoroughly depressed. I'd barely noticed the water growing colder by the minute. I was too wrapped up in thoughts of Inigo. Too busy being miserable. My gloomy thoughts were interrupted by a knock on the door.

Room service. My stomach rumbled as I started to clamber out of the bathtub and realized I was stuck. I couldn't move. The water around me had turned into a solid block of ice.

Chapter Seventeen

Thank gods for bathroom phones in good hotels. I snatched it off the wall and dialed Trevor's room even as my teeth began to chatter. When he picked up, he sounded half-asleep.

"You need to get a copy of my room key and get in here now," I snapped. I slammed the phone down without waiting for his response. Goose pimples had broken out pretty much everywhere, and I couldn't feel my legs.

I'd already turned on the hot water tap, but it wasn't cutting it. My body kept turning the water cool the minute it touched my skin. The ice simply wasn't melting fast enough, and the water level was already precariously close to spilling over the top of the tub. I had no choice but to turn off the taps.

Out of desperation, I grabbed the plastic shower curtain and yanked it from its hooks. It collapsed on me like it was going to smother the breath from my lungs. Panicked, I batted it away from my face and wrapped it around me as best I could. There was nothing I could do about the lower half of my body, currently encased in ice. I tried to call the Fire, but it was as if the powers inside me had gone to sleep. All I could do was wait.

At some point, the knocking on my door had stopped. Damn. There went my dinner plans. My stomach grumbled in protest.

I breathed a sigh of relief as I heard Trevor at the door. "Morgan?" he called.

"In the bathroom," I replied.

He stepped to the door, stopped, and stared. "What the hell?"

"Good question," I said, teeth chattering. "One m-minute I'm taking a bath, and the next my b-bathwater is frozen s-solid." I swished the curtain aside so he could see my legs in their ice block. It was like Han Solo on a really bad day.

"Call the Fire" he said, kneeling beside the tub.

"Y-you think I-I didn't try that?" I said testily. "Apparently, my powers have gone on vacation." Actually that didn't sound like a bad idea. Maybe I needed a vacation.

"This isn't a joke, Morgan," he said. "Your legs could get frostbite and be seriously damaged. You could even die."

"Gee, thanks f-for the p-pep talk. You think I h-haven't thought of that? I'm u-up to my waist in ice and w-worried about a lot more than j-just my legs."

His cheeks turned pink.

Trevor reached out and took my hands. "Let's try something," he said. "Close your eyes, take a deep breath, and focus on the Fire."

Like I hadn't done that at least a dozen times since I called him. I scowled, but did as he said. I didn't see how him holding my hands could help, but I went ahead and gave it a try. As I focused I could almost feel the energy Trevor was pouring down through my hands. The Fire inside me stirred sluggishly. I pulled at it harder, willing it to do something to get me out of this situation. It didn't. Instead, it seemed to curl up like a cat preparing to go back to sleep.

"Focus, Morgan," Trevor ordered. "The Fire *must* obey you. It is yours to command. Make it obey you."

That was easier said than done, but I took the energy Trevor was pouring into me and reached down inside me. I grabbed the Fire around its virtual throat and practically yanked it out of me. In a rush, it came roaring out, screaming in anger as it went. Trevor scrambled back out of the way. The Fire wouldn't harm me, but it could burn Trevor to a crisp.

The Fire lapped hungrily at the ice, irritated the frozen water didn't burn. I tossed the shower curtain away before it could melt and crossed my arms over my chest. I was less worried about being naked and more worried about being cold. Slowly the ice began to steam, then melt, and finally turned back into a pool of water. As soon as my legs were free, Trevor yanked me from the tub. I collapsed on top the shower curtain, naked ass in the air, shivering. The Fire continued to dance along my skin, warming me from the inside out. Luckily it didn't seem to affect the shower curtain for all that it was made of plastic. I guessed it must be one of those fire retardant materials. Three cheers for OSHA.

Trevor handed me a big fluffy towel to wrap myself in, then sat next to me on the tile. He stared at me for a full minute. "Let me guess," he said. "You're channeling Water now."

"That would be a big fat yes."

"Since when?"

I shrugged. "Not sure, but there's been some weird shit going on since the cruise ship. I think maybe it got activated being on the water." Or more likely, being near Eddie, although I'd been around him for months without a problem. Why now? Maybe it was Eddie being near the water and me being near Eddie... I shook my head. "The ice thing is new. Well, newish." I told him about killing the vampires on the island with icicles.

"I think it's time you took a trip to see Tommy," he said. His tone brooked no argument. I couldn't blame him. He'd just seen his sister frozen solid. I'd probably get all bossy and stuff, too.

"Oh, I plan to," I agreed. "It's just that we have more important things to deal with right now."

"What's more important than you controlling your powers? What's more important than your life?"

"Oh, I don't know," I said testily. "Saving the world maybe?"

"How are you going to save the world if you're dead?"

He had a point. I needed to get these powers under control before they destroyed me and everyone around me. But I also needed to stop Alister. "Fine. But who's going after Alister? He could be anywhere. We must find him."

"We will," he said. "I'll make sure of it. You go get your shit together."

Trust your brother to tell you how it is.

# # #

"It's about time you got here."

I grinned as I slammed the trunk of my vintage Mustang shut. Tommy Wahenaka had a way with words.

Tommy was a shaman for the Confederated Tribes of Warm Springs. He'd befriended my father, or rather, my

159

father's ghost. And he'd watched over Trevor while he was growing up. Now he was my Yoda. Only I'm pretty sure Yoda was more talkative and less bossy.

"You've been waiting for me, then?" It was a question I didn't really need to ask.

Tommy snorted. "Trouble follows you like flies follow horse pucky, kiddo," he said, leaning casually on his hand-carved walking stick. He was dressed from top to bottom in faded denim topped with a battered cowboy hat and a pair of scuffed boots badly in need of new soles. A long iron-colored braid hung down his back, and you could have made a road map out of the lines on his face. But his eyes...his eyes were beautiful, ageless, full of the mysteries of the universe. "It was only a matter of time."

"Gee. Your faith in me is overwhelming."

He didn't bother responding. Instead he took my bag and carried it into the cabin. I followed behind more slowly, taking in the view. Things hadn't changed much in Tommy's world. The cabin was still its rickety, rustic self. The land around was still the same juniper- and sagebrush-studded dustbowl. The sky above was still so blue it hurt my eyes, and the wind stirred up little dust devils that danced across the potholed drive. It took a rugged kind of person to make to make it in this desolate landscape. Tommy was just the man for the job.

He put me in the same bedroom I'd had on my last visit. It wasn't much bigger than a closet, and there was just enough room for a single bed and a tiny cupboard to store my suitcase.

The last time I was here had also been to train after a catastrophic power failure. Made me sound like some kind of machine or something, but the truth was, my powers had a tendency to get away from me. Just when I thought I had them licked, they'd do something crazy, like freezing me in the bathtub or burning a house down. Tommy was the only person I knew who could help me control them. Maybe because he was a shaman, or maybe because of his promise to my father.

Tommy followed me into the room and dumped my suitcase in the corner. "Let's get started."

"Right now?" I'd just been running around the Nevada desert. I was exhausted. Bone tired. The last thing I wanted to do was play with my powers.

"No time like the present."

With a sigh I followed him outside. No sense burning down his cabin, I guessed. I didn't think that would go over too well. I followed Tommy across, well, what I guess would be called a lawn, although that was being generous. It was more like a patch of dry earth speckled with dead grass. It was late spring, so the grass should have been green, but the high desert was having a dry spell. We crunched across the gravel drive and onto the open plains of the high desert. Wonderful. The perfect place to start a brush fire. That was all I needed, my face plastered across the six o'clock news.

"Um, Tommy" I said. "I don't think this is a good idea."

"You afraid you gonna light something on fire?" The thought seemed to amuse him.

"Well, yeah, actually. I do have to tendency to burn things down. The last time, I burned down a whole house."

He mulled that over. "Ain't the Fire that's out of control."

"I beg to differ." I was pretty sure I hadn't hallucinated that house burning down. I mean stranger things had happened, but two other people had been there. So either we'd all lost our minds, or I really had burned something down. I was going with the latter.

"You can beg all you want," Tommy said. "But ain't gonna change facts."

"Are you kidding? I was there, Tommy. I saw with my own eyes. Kabita was there. Haakon. They saw it too."

"Well, sure," Tommy said with a nod. "But they only saw part of it."

"What you mean?"

"Well." He squinted up at the sky, his forehead puckered in thought. "What they didn't see was you channeling Water until you nearly gave yourself hypothermia. *Then,* and only then, did you start burning things down. Bet that was a sight."

I stared at him for a moment. He was right. I'd worn myself out with the Water before I'd tried channeling Fire. By then I'd been so cold, I could hardly focus, and the Fire took over. I'd been too tired to control it. Too exhausted to focus. "How do you know what happened?"

He snorted, clearly amused by the question. "Ain't lived this long for nothing, girl."

"So, we're going to work on Water, then." Might as well resign myself to my fate.

He looked down at the dry earth and grinned. "Lawn could use some."

No kidding.

# # #

"Tell me about this Haakon fellow."

I paused, spoon halfway to my mouth. "Not much to tell." I shoveled in the stew and chomped blissfully. I wasn't really a stew person, but Tommy's was the stuff of legends. It was the best venison stew I'd ever tasted. It was the only venison stew I'd ever tasted, come to that.

Tommy simply raised an eyebrow as he chewed. I cleared my throat and tugged the rough wool blanket tighter around me. I was still bone-cold from the last two hours of exercises. Tommy could be a brutal taskmaster.

"Fine," I said. "According to Eddie, his name is Haakon Airik Magnussen. Once upon a time he was a Viking." I took another bite and nearly moaned as heat spread through my chilled body.

Tommy's brow went a little higher, but he still didn't say anything. I snagged another biscuit off the plate in the middle of the table. Anything to delay the inevitable. Tommy waited.

I sighed. "He's a Sunwalker. Like Jack."

Tommy made a sound that was halfway between a grunt and a snort. I wasn't sure what it meant, so I ignored him and munched on my biscuit.

"I know what you want me to say," I said finally.

Tommy said nothing, just gave me a look and kept eating. Tommy could say a whole lot without saying anything at all.

"You want me to admit I'm a Sunwalker too." I stabbed viciously at a piece of potato.

"Do I?"

"Everyone else does."

"Do they?"

I gave irritated growl. "Everyone says I'm a Sunwalker," I snapped. "Jack. Darroch."

"Ah, yes. Brent Darroch is exactly the sort of man you should listen to." His sarcasm was not lost on me.

"What about Jack? He wouldn't lie to me."

"No. But he sees what he wishes to see."

"Are you saying I'm not a Sunwalker?" Because if he was, he was just about the first person to say so.

"Didn't say that."

My heart sank. "So, I am one."

"Didn't say that either."

I wanted to scream in frustration. It was a regular state of affairs with Tommy. Seriously, he had the enigma thing down pat. "What am I then?"

"Who do you think you are?" He didn't say it a confrontational way. More like in a vaguely interested way, as if I was some sort of scientific experiment. Okay, that wasn't fair. Tommy wasn't like that. But still, it didn't seem like he was invested in my answer, only curious to see what I would come up with.

"I don't know," I said finally.

"That's the smartest thing I've ever heard you say." He stood up and began clearing the dishes from the table. "Now, let's go practice."

"Again?" Every muscle in my body already ached, my brain was exhausted, and I was only just recovering from the cold. I didn't think I could take much more.

"Sun's not down yet," he said. "Plenty of time left."

I groaned. It would be a miracle if I made it through the day alive.

Chapter Eighteen

Three days went by with no word of Alister. Wherever he was, he was definitely keeping a low profile. In the meantime, Tommy was beating the proverbial shit out of me with his exercise drills. I didn't know that I was getting any better at controlling Water, but I hadn't frozen myself to death again. I supposed that was a good sign.

From dawn until dusk, and even sometimes well into the night, Tommy had me calling my powers. Sometimes he'd have me use one until I'd nearly exhausted it. Sometimes he'd ask me to bounce back and forth between different powers or use two of them together. Other times he had me call them all at once, weaving them together into one powerful weapon. Or at least, that was the goal. I'd yet to succeed even once at that one.

We were about to head out for another session of Beat-up-on-Morgan when my cell phone rang. I breathed a sigh of relief until I saw it was Jack. I'd almost rather face Tommy's endless drills.

"Well, look what the cat dragged in."

There was a pause. "Excuse me?" Jack's tone was stilted. Dude seriously needed to loosen up.

"Never mind," I said. "What's up?"

"I think I might have a lead on Alister."

Finally. "Michigan?"

A moment of silence. "Why Michigan?"

"Jade thought he might be there. He talked about it."

"Pretty sure he is not in Michigan," Jack said. "My sources say he somewhere in—get this—Scotland."

"You have got to be kidding me." All this, and Alister was in Dragon territory? A man who hated dragons with a passion?

"It's odd, right? It was the last place I expected him to be."

Something niggled at my brain. "Jade said something about Alister going to hide the book in the last place anyone would expect it to be. Somewhere totally obvious."

"How is Scotland obvious?" he asked. "That's more like the exact opposite of obvious."

He was right, which was what was so confusing. Obvious would've been back in London. MI8 maybe. Not in the middle of the land owned by his enemies. The dragons were not going to like Alister in their territory. Drago was going to go batshit when he found out. Which was why he was the last person on the planet I planned on telling.

"You're sure he's there?" I asked.

"As sure as I can be," Jack said. "I'm headed there now. I'll let you know what I find out."

"Okay, keep me posted." I hung up the phone, stared at it a minute, then shoved it back in my pocket.

"I take it you're going to Scotland." Tommy's face was devoid of expression. I couldn't tell if he was pleased, angry, or just didn't care.

"I have to."

"Because of Inigo." Still no expression.

He was right, of course. I wanted to say it was because I was going to save the world, or because I planned to catch Alister. Those things were true. But the truth was, I'd use any excuse to see Inigo again. Even if he didn't want to see me. How pathetic was that?

166

I didn't say any of that, of course. "I have to go, Tommy."

He nodded. As I walked away I felt his eyes on me all the way to the cabin.

# # #

The irony of Alister choosing Scotland as a hideout did not escape me. I'd never been one to believe in coincidences, and this was far beyond mere coincidence. Alister and his ancestors had done everything they could to eradicate the Dragon race. Alister himself had told me how much he hated them. He wanted one race and one race only on this planet: humans. I'm not even sure I'd pass muster at this point. He was willing to use any means necessary—even supernatural ones—to ensure the supernatural races were wiped out.

What was he doing in Scotland? What did he have planned? Whatever it was, he couldn't possibly be up to any good.

Jack met me at the train station in Edinburgh. I quickly picked him out in the crowd. He stood head and shoulders above the rest, his longish hair kissed by the sun, and his eyes the color of the ocean just before a storm. Men gave him a wide berth. Women ogled him with unconcealed lust. Couldn't say I blamed them. He was one fine specimen of manhood. Unfortunately, he was as messed up in the head as the rest of them.

I joined him on the platform. "Anything new?"

He shook his head as he led me toward the exit. "Still looking. Turns out he owns a couple of flats on the Royal

Mile. According to my sources, he was staying in one, but by the time I got there, the place was empty."

"And no leads to where he might've gone?"

"Not one." Frustration colored his tone. It looked like he hadn't slept in a few days. His edginess was almost palpable, and it was making me cranky.

"Okay," I said. "I'd like to see the place for myself."

"You think I missed something?" He sounded offended. Stupid man and his gods-awful pride. Made me want to smack him upside the head.

"Maybe. Maybe not. But a second set of eyes never hurts." I wasn't about to downplay how serious this was to sooth his wounded ego. I had a job to do.

"Fine," he ground out. "Car's over there."

He led me to a small, dirty blue Fiat parked on the street near the train station. It was one of the ugliest damn cars I'd ever seen, but we were sure to blend in fine. With Alister, our only chance was if he never saw us coming. After storing my bag in the trunk, or boot, as they called it there, I slid into the passenger seat on the left side of the car. Jack started the engine and pulled out into traffic.

The train station wasn't far from the Royal Mile, so it wasn't long before we were pulling into a small private car park. Leaving my bag in the car, Jack led me the few blocks to Alister's flat. It was a modest second floor walk-up, which surprised me. I'd expected a penthouse suite or something fancier, not this humble one-bedroom with the world's smallest kitchenette.

Jack lingered inside the door while I prowled around the apartment. There wasn't much to see: no pictures on the walls, no food in the fridge, no toiletries in the bathroom. The only thing left in the wardrobe was a single wire hanger. I even checked under the bed and behind the fridge; nothing but dust bunnies.

I stood in the middle of the living room and turned slowly in a circle. The sagging couch was at least ten years old and the TV not much newer. There was a cheap, flat, pack-end table with a brass lamp that looked like it had come from a thrift shop. The dented lampshade had once been cream, but was now a dirty beige. I lifted the couch cushions and found a single copper pence and a couple stale pieces of popcorn. I let the cushions fall back into place with a sigh.

"There's absolutely nothing here."

Jack shrugged as if to say "Told you." It's a good thing he didn't say it out loud, or I might have slugged him. His attitude lately had been testing my patience.

"Not helpful, Jack." I moved into the bedroom and stared at the bed, frowning. I lifted the duvet, and a small puff of dust rose into the air. Letting it fall back into place, I strode back into the front room. "He was never here. Alister was never in this apartment."

Jack frowned. "What do you mean?"

"I know some of you men aren't big on cleanliness," I said. "But even you must've noticed there's way too much dust here. The bed hasn't been slept in. That TV—" I stabbed a finger in the direction of the set—" is way out of date. The entire UK went digital years ago. It wouldn't even receive a signal now. This is all...set dressing."

"What are you talking about?"

"Nobody lives here, Jack. Nobody even stays here. I don't know how Alister convinced your 'sources' he was holing up here, but I'll bet anything he never set foot in this place."

"My sources wouldn't lie." Jack's jaw was clenched, a sure sign he was pissed.

"Not saying they did. I'm saying they were fooled. Alister tricked them. I don't know how, but he was never in this building."

"Fine. So where is he?"

I shook my head. "No idea. But I'll bet he's nowhere near Scotland." Jade had said the place would be so obvious, I wouldn't expect it. And while I hadn't expected Scotland, it wasn't an obvious place either. It felt all wrong.

Jack let out a growl of frustration and slammed his fist against the wall. The lath and plaster cracked under the impact. I wanted to say something snarky, but I bit my tongue. No point getting him more riled up than he already was.

"Now what?" Jack snarled.

He was asking me? That was a first. "I say you go back to your sources and see what you can dig up."

"And you?"

"I've got a Dragon to visit."

Chapter Nineteen

For a guy who liked to wear worn jeans and black leather jackets, Drago's office was surprisingly elegant. The walls were covered in bookshelves stuffed with leather-bound volumes. The plush carpet was the color of port wine, and the massive oak desk was stained almost black. I wasn't surprised to note that the intricately carved legs were dragons. Everywhere I looked were dragons: dragon statuettes in niches, dragon tapestries hanging from the walls. There was an even a little pewter box on Drago's desk with a dragon perched on top'.

"Overkill on the dragon theme, don't you think?"

He rolled his eyes. "People seem to think because I'm the king of the dragons, I need a bunch of dragon shit. What else am I supposed to do with it? Do you know what kind of a bollocking I would get if one of the dukes walked in and their gift wasn't on display?"

"Good point." I sank into one of the cushy chairs opposite him.

"What can I do for you, Morgan?" Tilting back in his chair, he propped his booted feet on the massive desk. He looked more like a cover model for a romance novel than royalty. "If it's about Inigo, not much I can do there." He sounded like he was sorry about that. I didn't blame him. You can't make people do stuff they don't want to do, and I seriously doubted Inigo was open to his brother meddling.

"I know. It's not that. It's Alister Jones."

"What's that asshole up to now?"

A smiled tugged at my lips. "He's in the wind. Still. We almost had him in the Caribbean, but he got away. Jack got a lead that he was in Edinburgh, but when we got there, we found no trace of him. Pretty sure it was a deliberately false lead."

"How can I help?" He steepled his fingers and stared at me with inscrutable gold eyes.

"Rumor has it you have a network of, ah, informants," I said.

He raised an eyebrow. I couldn't tell if he was surprised or upset that I knew. "Who told you that?"

The truth was, no one had, but it made sense. You don't become the leader of your people if you don't have the smarts to gather the knowledge to keep them safe. Especially if your species has been hunted for centuries. The only way to stop an egomaniac out to kill you is to get in front of him. To have better information than he has. To know what he's going to do before he does it.

"Does it matter? Point is, I know, and I need your help stopping Alister."

He tilted back little farther and stared up at the ceiling for a moment. "I'll send out some feelers, let you know what I find. "

"Thanks." I started to get up, but his next words stopped me.

"As for Inigo. I know you're hoping things will change," he said. "But they might not. I told you when we started this whole thing he might never be the same."

What he'd told me was that Inigo might not survive, but he had. "He's alive," I said. "That's what matters."

"Is it?"

172

I shook my head and gave him a weak smile before striding from the room. It had to be. I refused to believe it would have been better if I'd let him die.

#

My footsteps slowed as I reached the door to Inigo's room. Part of me was eager to see him again, but a bigger part of me was terrified by what I'd find. I dreaded another run-in with the cold, hard man he'd become. That was not the Inigo I knew and loved. That was not the man who held me when I needed it and kicked me in the butt when I needed that. I felt guilty, but he was a stranger, and I really didn't want to see him again. I wanted my Inigo back. That was the truth. I wasn't sure what I'd do if the stranger was there again. Tanith had told me to be patient, to wait. I wasn't sure I had it in me. I wasn't sure my heart wouldn't break long before he healed.

Telling myself to grow a freaking backbone, I stepped to the open doorway. He was sitting in a chair next to the window, the sunlight shining on his golden hair. He was wearing clothes too, not just pajamas. I couldn't help but feel a little thrill of hope. Clearly, he was getting better. Physically, at least.

"Inigo?" I hated the hesitation in my voice and the butterflies in my stomach. This was ridiculous. He was my boyfriend. I shouldn't be afraid to see him, talk to him. And yet I was.

He turned slightly until his eyes caught mine. Those beautiful blue eyes that had once looked at me with such love, such passion. At least this time they weren't cold.

"Morgan." His tone was neutral. I couldn't tell if he was happy to see me, angry, or what. Maybe he just didn't care. I shoved that thought aside. I could take anything but that.

"I wanted to see how you're doing," I said, pausing at the foot of the bed. I could smell him, a chocolatey campfire scent tinged with vanilla that was his alone. I wanted to wrap my arms around him and breathe him in, but instead I wrapped my hand around the bedpost and clung to it for dear life.

Inigo glanced out the window as if he found the sweeping green lawn behind the castle fascinating. "Better," he said.

"That's good." I didn't know what else to say. He wasn't exactly encouraging, but at least there wasn't that cold anger. I didn't think I could've handled that. "It's good to see you out of bed."

He shrugged. "Guess I was getting tired of lying around."

It wasn't exactly a joke, but I'd take it. Since he wasn't yelling at me to leave him alone, I perched on the edge of the bed. I felt awkward, out of place. I had no idea what to say. The sad thing was, Inigo and I had always had things talk about, and suddenly there was nothing. I reminded myself to be thankful the emotionless stranger seemed to be gone. Awkwardness I could deal with. If I had to.

Inigo cleared his throat. "So what's been going on? Catch me up." He tried to keep his tone light, but I could tell it was a struggle. I guessed we were going with the whole "pretend everything's normal" thing.

I gave him a quick rundown on my trip to the Caribbean, complete with vampires and Alister Jones. I told him about my new power, my training with Tommy, the visit to Nevada and Jade, and everything we'd done so far to try and find Alister. I didn't mention Haakon. I'm not sure why. It wasn't like there was anything going on with us, but something kept me from telling Inigo about the Viking Sunwalker.

"Sounds exciting," he said dryly.

"Oh, you know me," I said. "A thrill a minute."

There was another awkward pause, punctuated only by the hum of a hedge trimmer from below. The castle came with some very nice gardens, if the view from Inigo's window was anything to go by.

I cleared my throat. "You? Anything exciting?"

"The usual. Physical therapy, mental bullshit. Drago's been by a few times to help me with my Dragon abilities."

That surprised me. I hadn't realized the healing coma had affected that part of him. "Really? Has it been helpful?" Gods, the awkwardness was killing me.

"Yeah," he said. "I've actually been able to shift a couple times."

"That's good," I said lamely. I didn't know what else to say. But if he could shift to his Dragon form, that had to be a good sign, right?

"Tanith says I can go home soon." His tone was completely neutral. No indication as to whether he considered this a good or bad thing. Whether he wanted to go or stay. No excitement. No happiness. But no sadness either.

"Great!" I forced a cheerfulness I didn't feel. "So, you really must be on the mend. Are you looking forward to going home?" When in doubt, just confront the question head-on. Even if the answer hurt like hell.

Inigo shrugged. "Guess so. It's time. Can't bum around here the rest of my life." It sounded like it was something he'd actually considered.

"So, um, when do you plan to fly back to Portland?" And were we still together? And did he still love me? But I didn't ask those questions because I really didn't want to know the answers. I had a feeling I might not like what he had to say.

"Next week."

I forced a smile. "I could pick you up at the airport."

"Sure." He didn't sound terribly enthusiastic, but I'd take what I could get.

"Fantastic. Text me with your flight info," I said, standing up. "It was good to see you."

He nodded, but didn't say he was happy to see me. I tried not to take it personally, but it was almost impossible not to. I gave him another forced smile and strode from the room, keeping my back ramrod straight. I waited until I was safely in the car with the doors locked before I let the tears fall.

Shéa MacLeod

Chapter Twenty

I spent the next week in a constant state of near panic. I could hardly eat. I could barely sleep. And if Kabita's snarky comments were anything to go by, I'd turned into a raving bitch. I was so anxious about Inigo's impending return to Portland, I couldn't seem to focus on anything. With Jack and Trevor off hunting Alister, and Kabita swamped with paperwork, I was left to do the usual: hunt vampires. Vamps didn't take the night off because I was feeling out of sorts.

Shortly before midnight, I pushed my way through the doors of Fringe. A visit to the nightclub popular with the supernatural set had not been in my original plan, but driving along the dark streets of Portland, I'd had the sudden inspiration to visit my friend, Cordelia. Maybe her clairvoyant talents were the key we needed to solve the puzzle of Alister.

The club was dark inside, lit only by dim red lights along the walls and the blue neon behind the bar. The occasional strobe lit up the dance floor, highlighting the writhing bodies dancing in the dark. Cordelia's alcove was on the other side of the dance floor, so I pushed my way into the heaving crowd. I had made it to the middle of the floor when I found myself being half-molested by a shape shifter. I wasn't sure what kind he was, but I was guessing some sort of cat from the way he was rubbing himself all over me. His eyes flashed gold in the next strobe, and I swear to the gods, I heard him purr. He smelled of musk and green, living things. The scent swirled around me, tangling my senses. He slid a hand down my body, coming perilously close to my lady parts.

I grabbed his hand and jerked it away with a glare that had made vampires quail. His eyes widened as he pulled free and backed away, palms toward me in the sign of universal surrender. I waved him off and pushed my way through the crowd toward the alcove where Cordelia Nightwing held court.

The shimmering silver privacy curtain was slightly open, which told me she was available. I slipped through the opening and plopped myself in the chair opposite her. She glanced up from her tarot cards with a smile, blue eyes dancing with merriment.

"I see Lothario got to you."

I snorted. "That's not seriously his name, is it?"

She laughed, her eyes crinkling at the corners. "I doubt it, but that's what everyone calls him. More than one woman has fallen under his spell." She tucked a dark lock of hair behind one ear.

"No way. You?" Cordy didn't seem the type to fall for an over-hormonal cat shifter.

"What can I say?" she said, with a slight tilt of her head. "He was amazing in bed."

"Ew. TMI. I hope you checked for fleas afterward." It was snarky and mean, but it was how I was feeling. The guy had dry-humped me in the middle of a nightclub. That shit was reserved for one man and one man only.

"Well, somebody's a cranky pants," Cordelia said as she shuffled her tarot deck. She was wearing a bright red silk kimono embroidered with gold dragons and a matching turban wrapped around her dark hair. She always claimed she dressed like that so as not to disappoint her customers, but I was pretty sure she just liked wearing kimonos.

I snorted. "You'd be cranky too, if you were in my shoes."

She eyed me carefully. "Problems?"

She didn't need her spirit guides to tell her that. "The usual. We almost had that bastard, Alister, but he's in the wind again. Every time we have a lead, it turns into nothing. Drago's got his people working on it, but..." I shook my head.

"Have you considered scrying for him?"

I could have smacked myself in the head. Scrying had never entered my mind. I didn't know why. I worked for a Witch, after all, but I was used to a more direct approach. "Uh, no. Can you do it?"

She shook her head. "Not my thing. You need a Witch for that. I'm surprised Kabita hasn't suggested it."

I was too, now I thought of it, but then Kabita tended to be pretty low key about witchy stuff. "I'll ask her."

"What else is on your mind?" Cordelia asked, eyes on my face. "Let me guess. Boyfriend problems." Nothing slipped passed her.

I heaved a sigh. "Yeah. Still. I mean, things are better. At least he doesn't openly hate me anymore, but he still acts like I'm some kind of stranger. Cold, you know?"

"This is normal for his condition?"

"I guess." I shrugged. "Tanith says I need to give him time."

"Tanith would know."

I wondered, not for the first time, about Cordelia's relationship with her sister. It wasn't like they hated each

179

other, but more like they were, well, strangers. Not unlike Inigo and me at the moment. Talk about depressing.

"I don't suppose the cards have anything to say on the matter?" I asked. It was what I'd come for, after all.

Cordelia shot me a smile and held out the deck. It was an old one, well worn, with richly colored illustrations in swirling blues and greens. I slid my fingers over the deck, the paper worn smooth from handling, chose three cards, and laid them face-down on the table. She turned the first one over and made a humming sound. She raised her eyebrow as she turned over the second. On turning over the third, she said, "Interesting."

That didn't sound good. "What is it?" I asked.

She tapped the first card with her long, crimson fingernail. "I don't need to tell you much about this card," she said. "It represents the past, and you know what your past with Inigo was."

I nodded. I was painfully aware.

"And this one," she said, tapping the second card. It was the eight of swords. "I don't think I need to tell you about this one, either. Right now you're feeling despair. A lack of hope. You feel trapped, and you don't know what to do."

No shit. I didn't need magic cards to tell me that.

She laid her hand gently on the third card. Three of swords. "This one isn't...great," she said, cautiously. "If you're not careful, you could open yourself up to a lot of pain."

"Too late."

"Now, Morgan," she said, grabbing my hand and giving it a squeeze. "It looks bad, I admit, but there is hope. Yes, if things stay the same, he will break your heart. But you have a choice. There are always choices. There *is* a way."

A way for what exactly? To be happy? If it meant leaving Inigo, I wasn't sure I was prepared for that. Although I might not have much choice in the matter. You can't make somebody love you again no matter how much you want them to. Sometimes all you can do is let go.

I was about to say something when a sudden gripping on the back of my skull distracted me. Vampire. Close. Like, in the club close. I pulled my hand from Cordelia's. "Thanks, Cordy. I appreciate it. I'll give it some thought." I rose from the table in a rush. "I've got to go."

"Please don't be sad," she said. She stood up and wrapped me in a warm hug. "I promise you. Things are going to come out right. They always do."

I wished I had her faith.

# # #

I slipped through the silver curtain back onto the crowded dance floor. Ignoring the press of scantily clad writhing bodies, I pushed my way around the edge of the dance floor. If there really was a vamp in the club, I needed to find it. Fast.

About halfway around the room, that gripping press on the back of my skull intensified. I froze in my tracks. Definitely close. I still couldn't figure out how a vamp had gotten into Fringe. The mysterious owner of the club and his trusty bartender would never allow that. Fringe might freely welcome all supernaturals, but that didn't extend to vamps or anyone else likely to cause trouble. There were wards on the doors to prevent such things from entering. In fact, they were the strongest wards I'd ever seen. Whoever had placed them must be one hell of a Witch. How had a vampire gotten past the wards?

Focusing on the pressure in my head, I stepped cautiously to the left toward the bar. The pressure eased up. Okay, not that direction. I continued my circuit around the room toward the exit at the front of the club. Again, the pressure grew fainter. Right, then. The vamp was somewhere on the right side of the room on the other side of the dance floor.

Sinking down on an empty barstool, I scanned the edge of the room as casually as possible. No one stood out, but that didn't mean anything. In a place like this, everyone looked a little...inhuman.

A trio of sidhe drifted by, their faces an ever-changing morph of features. The constant shift coupled with the strobe lights was downright nausea-inducing. The three of them ignored me, which was odd. Every sidhe in existence knew who I was. What was Morgana up to?

I eyed a gentleman in one corner. He was dressed in a snazzy black suit with a shiny silver tie. There were three different women draped all over him while several more hovered, entranced by his every word. I narrowed my eyes. Could be the vamp. He was excessively pale. But vampires didn't care about sex. They only cared about feeding. Blood. A vamp might select one person to entrance, but only so he could get her out of the club as quickly as possible. He would not collect an entire harem of fawning women. Nor would he be as clearly aroused by the attention as this man appeared to be. I axed Snazzy Suit off my list.

182

"What can I get you, miss?"

I swiveled on my stool to face the bartender—Axel, I believe his name was. He hadn't raised his voice. He hadn't needed to. I could hear him easily over the loud thumping music, and he knew it. I eyeballed him carefully. His shoulder length brown hair was pulled back in a queue and thick muscles rippled beneath his simple black T-shirt. He could have passed for ordinary, but his eyes gave him away. The icy blue orbs where anything but human. Wolf's eyes. I bowed my head a little, and he acknowledged with a wink. He knew what I was, and I knew what he was. We were cool. What I didn't know was if he realized he had a vamp running amok in his nightclub. I doubted it. He seemed far too calm. His kind wasn't known for calm where vamps were concerned.

"Just a ginger ale, thanks." Getting drunk was the last thing I needed. Hard to hunt vamps when you're three sheets to the wind, but I needed a prop to avert suspicion.

Axel shook his head and grabbed a glass. Filling it with ice, he added ginger ale and a twist of lime, and slid the glass across the counter. I started to pull out my wallet, but he stopped me.

"Hunters drink free," he said, his voice a low rumble I could feel in my chest. "Especially when they're on the hunt. You should know that by now."

So he did know there was a vamp in the club. Or at least he knew I was hunting one, which pretty much amounted to the same thing.

"How did a vamp get past the wards?" I didn't raise my voice, either. He could hear me as easily as I heard him. Super hearing has its benefits.

He carefully wiped down the counter in front of me with a white bar towel. "No idea. Somebody with magic and a knowledge of the wards had to have let it through."

Shit. That wasn't good. "Any idea who that would be?"

"Lot of people know about the wards."

It was true. Anyone who walked through the door would feel them. I changed tack.

"Have you seen him?" I asked, taking a sip of my ginger ale.

"I'm guessing that's him." Axel nodded ever so slightly toward the back door. "Or, rather, her."

I turned around cautiously, not wanting to alert my prey. I spotted the vamp instantly. She was barely dressed in a shiny silver lamé thing with matching stilettos studded in rhinestones. More pale skin on display than cloth. Her white-blonde hair hung nearly to her waist as she sashayed toward the exit, showing off just a hint of cheek with every stride. It was a good thing she waxed before she died. She pulled a young man along behind her. He looked barely legal. His eyes were wide as if he couldn't believe what was happening. He really wasn't gonna believe it when she sank her fangs in his neck. They stepped outside, and the door slammed shut behind them.

"Thanks," I said, hopping off the barstool. I didn't wait for the Axel's reply, but headed across the floor toward the back exit. I must've looked like a woman on a mission because no one bothered me this time. In fact, people seemed to be in an inordinate hurry to get out of my way. Fine with me.

As I approached the door, I pulled my machete from the sheath across my back. When in Portland, I pretty much went everywhere with it. Tonight that certainly proved to be a good policy.

Cautiously, I pushed open the exit door and peered around the corner. I spotted the pair next to a rather smelly dumpster, writhing and moaning like a couple of animals in heat. They looked like they were necking, but I could smell the copper tang of blood. Shit. I was already too late. If I grabbed the vamp, she'd rip the kid's throat out. I needed to make her let go willingly. How to do that? I grinned as a thought came to me. I stepped outside, closing the door cautiously behind me so as not to alert the vampire.

"Here vampy, vampy," I called in a singsong voice, tapping my blade against the metal fire door. The metallic sound rang off the brick walls, echoing in the narrow alley.

The vamp lifted her head from her prey and snarled at me. Bright red blood dripped from her fangs and coated her mouth in a grotesque lipstick. It really wasn't her color.

"Oh, I'm scared." Sarcasm dripped from my voice as I launched the childish taunt.

She let the boy go. He fell against the dumpster with a thud and slumped to the ground. In the glow of a nearby streetlight he looked paler than he should. Not a good sign. I needed to get him help, but first things first. Vamp girl hissed at me like an angry cat, her eyes glowing red in the dim light. Interesting. She was clearly under the control of someone who wasn't a vampire. Was she, perhaps, a soul vamp? One of Alister's making maybe?

"Please," I snapped. "Is that all you've got? Pathetic. Kaldan would have been so ashamed." Kaldan had once ruled all the vamps in Portland. Until I'd separated his head

185

from his body. I was betting he'd held her reins once upon a time.

With a howl of rage, the vampire flew at me. She moved so fast, I barely had time to slice her with my machete. She hit me hard, and I fell with a *thump*, flat on my back. The wind whooshed out of my lungs. For a moment I lay there, stunned, unable to move. She reared back, fangs bared, going for my throat. I managed to roll my head to the side enough that she hit my shoulder instead. The pain of her fangs sinking into my flesh was like fire ripping through my body. That was definitely going to leave a mark.

My machete was pinned under her left knee. Only thing I could do was haul off and punch her in the temple with my fist. She pulled back, surprised by my move. Her scream of rage nearly deafened me as blood and spit sprayed across my face. Gross.

I bucked my hips, dislodging her just enough to free my machete. It was too close quarters for the weapon, so I gave her another good bash against the head with the handle, throwing her off me. Something crunched, and her scream of rage turned to one of pain as I opened up a good six-inch gash along her temple. The blow probably would've killed a human.

I staggered to my feet as the vamp pressed her hand against the gash, trying to stem the flow of blood, but I could see the sticky dark liquid still pouring between her fingers. Since she'd eaten recently, the blood was flowing faster than normal, but it was still darker and more viscous than human blood. She scrambled away from me, glancing back toward the inert body of the young man. I knew what she was thinking. If she could only get to the boy, she could feed and her body would heal that much faster. No way would I let that happen. It was time to practice what Tommy had been training me to do. See if I could wield my new power without succumbing to it.

I needed to find out how she'd gotten through the wards. Could I use my powers to restrain rather than kill? Time to find out.

Without hesitation I pulled on the Water within me. It came quickly, eagerly. No surprise there. All of my powers liked to get out and play from time to time.

As I called it, the Water began to pool in the center of my hand. Sending my mental energy into the cupped water, I hurled it at the vampire. As it left my hand, the water turned to ice. The vamp's eyes widened, and she tried to move out of the way, but it was too late. The dagger-shaped shard of ice lodged in her breast, a fraction from her heart. She stared down at it in horror, then up at me. I breathed a sigh of relief. Talk about a close call. If she so much as moved, the shard would hit her heart, and she'd be a goner. I really needed to practice my aim.

I half expected the icicle in her chest to start melting, but it didn't. It glittered beneath the streetlight, cold and deadly.

I strode toward her with a smile. Fear was written all over her face. Definitely a soul vamp. Regular vamps didn't feel fear.

"What are you?" she whispered, her voice wobbling a bit.

I cocked my head to the side. Water was still riding me. I could feel it swirling, cold and dark, in my soul. "I am Hunter," I said.

"No." Her voice was so faint I had to strain to hear it. "You are more. There is ice in your eyes."

I wasn't sure what that meant, but I wasn't here for a personal appraisal. "How did you get past the wards?" I demanded.

"It doesn't matter."

"Do you want to be free?"

She stared at me, eyes wide. "Yes."

"Then tell me."

She swallowed. "I can't."

Shit. Whoever her master was had given her an order she wouldn't be able to break. "Who is your master?"

She shook her head. "I can't tell you that, either."

"Give me something."

"There is nothing I can tell you. Except that none of this, none of it is by chance. I'm sorry."

"I don't—" But before I could finish the sentence, she twisted to the right. I knew the minute the shard hit her heart; between one breath and the next, she exploded in a cloud of dust and ash.

I stared at the small pile of ash for a moment, then turned and hurried to the boy. He was deathly pale, and his breathing was shallow. His pulse was weak and erratic. I had no idea how I was going explain this to anyone, but the kid needed a hospital fast.

I shrugged out of my jacket and yanked my T-shirt up over my head. I pulled my jacket back on, zipped up, and then pressed my T-shirt against the wound on the boy's neck to stem the flow of blood. With the other hand, I pulled my phone out of my jeans pocket and dialed 911. Then I settled down to wait and make up my story.

About a minute later, I heard the faint sound of sirens in the distance. The back door of the club swung open, and Axel stuck his head out. His eyes glowed eerily for a moment, and then the glow was gone.

"You need to get out of here before the cops arrive," he said.

"Can't." I shook my head. "If I take pressure off this wound, this kid is going to die." I could not let that happen. I'd seen far too many people die because of the vamps. This kid wasn't going to be one of them. Not if I could help it.

"Fine," he growled, stomping outside and letting the door swing shut behind him. He knelt beside me and placed his hand over mine. "I've got this," he said. "Go. I promise not to let him die. Bad for business, you know."

With a nod, I pulled my hand out from under his, letting him take over. He was right. He was used to dealing with the cops, and I couldn't get involved in this. There was too much at stake. With a last glance at the pale form huddled on the ground, I slipped into the night and let the shadows take me.

Chapter Twenty-one

I slumped into the guest chair across from Kabita's desk. Slouching down, I slung one leg over the arm and swung it back and forth. "Cordelia says we should scry for Alister," I said casually. I eyed her closely. She was wearing a cute little pair of black-rimmed cat's eye glasses. They suited her warm skin and exotic looks marvelously, but I'd never seen her wear glasses before. "When did you get those?"

"Well, good afternoon to you too," she said dryly as she shuffled through a stack of papers on her desk. "I'm fine, thanks. How are you?"

I rolled my eyes. "Fine, whatever. I'm great. How are you, Kabita? Good morning. Now, glasses?"

She studied the papers in front of her a little more intently than necessary. "The doctor says I need them for reading." She shrugged as if it was no big deal. "Now, can we get down to business? What's this about scrying?"

"Alister. Cordy thinks we should try scrying for him. Can you do it?"

"No."

I blinked. That was unexpected. "Excuse me?"

She sighed and leaned in her chair. The leather squeaked in protest. "I'm too close, Morgan. Whatever I may think of him, he is my father."

"So what? You can't scry for family?"

She shook her head. "It's not that exactly. But in this case, there's too much... emotion involved." She meant anger. Betrayal.

"Ah," I said, swinging my foot a little bit harder. "It's 'cause you're pissed as hell at him, right?"

She gave me a wry smile and slid her glasses off. "Something like that. Besides, we would need something personal of my father's in order to scry for his location. I don't have anything like that."

I cleared my throat. "I do," I reminded her.

Her eyes narrowed. "The letter opener?"

"He was playing with it at the pink house while we were talking. It's real silver, too, with his initials engraved on it. Pretty sure that counts as personal."

She sighed as she pinched the bridge of her nose. "Okay. I guess it has to be done. I do know someone who might be able to help you."

I tried to raise one eyebrow, but both went up. Stupid, uncooperative eyebrows. "Someone from your coven?" I knew very well Kabita was a solitary witch. Covens weren't really her thing. Although she would visit one from time to time, she preferred to practice on her own.

"Not mine, a new one. The leader moved to Portland recently. But she's good. Real good. I'll text you her number."

I nodded and started to get up, but her next words stopped me.

"Have you been sleeping?"

"Why do you ask?"

She gave me a look as she slid her glasses back on. "You look tired."

"Gee, thanks," I said. "You really know how to make a girl feel special. I'm fine. Really." But it was a lie, and we

191

both knew it.

#

"Thanks for picking me up."

"No problem." I glanced at Inigo out of the corner of my eye. He was finally back in Portland with me where he belonged, and yet nothing felt as it should. Although that cold, bitter Inigo I'd first seen at the castle was gone, things were still awkward between us. Like two kids on a first date who didn't quite speak the same language. I didn't know what I could do or say to make it better.

"Kabita hired someone to clean your place," I blurted. I wanted to smack myself in the head. Before...everything, Inigo and I had practically been living together. We'd spent almost every night at my place. Or rather, almost every day, since I tended to work nights. He still kept his apartment in the Northwest District near 23rd Ave, the place I was taking him now. With things the way they were, taking him back to my place, while I would've preferred it, felt wrong. I knew in my heart of hearts he wouldn't have gone for it so I didn't try. I guess I didn't want to face certain rejection.

"That's nice." It didn't sound like he thought it was nice. It sounded like he didn't give a shit. He certainly wasn't urging me to take him to my place instead. I'd admit it. That hurt.

"Don't want to lose you amidst all those dust bunnies." The joke fell flat, so I focused on driving. It was probably the safest option. Both for the car and for my heart. The rest of the trip passed in silence.

Fifteen painful minutes later, I pulled up in front of Inigo's apartment building. I started to get out of the car. "Let me help you with your bags," I said.

"No! I don't need your help. Stop babying me. I'm not some sort of invalid." The words snapped out in sharp, ugly blotches that lacerated my heart. I cringed away from them. From him.

"Sorry," I said. I shut the door and sat staring at the steering wheel. I didn't want to look at him and see that same harsh ugliness in his eyes, staining his soul. "I know you've been through a lot. I'll just give you some space."

He heaved a heavy sigh. "I'm sorry, Morgan. You didn't deserve that. You don't deserve any of this."

I almost protested, but then gave myself a mental head slap. He was right. I didn't deserve it. I wasn't the one who'd hurt him. I was the one who'd stood by and loved him.

"I agree," I said. "I think I deserve a little respect. I think I deserve to be treated like a human being instead of shit on the bottom of your shoe." I turned and looked him straight in the eye. "I deserve to be treated like someone you love. That is, if you still love me." When in doubt, rip the Band-Aid off and pray to the gods you don't bleed to death.

He swallowed. "Of course I love you," he said. "I just... I need..." He shook his head.

"Space," I finished for him.

He nodded. "Yeah. Sorry." I could tell from the tone of his voice even he thought that was lame.

"Okay, then," I said turning back to stare through the windshield. My gut was churning, and my heart had fallen to somewhere in the vicinity of my toes. "I've got a psychopath to find so I'll see you later, all right?"

193

Inigo nodded and climbed out of the car. Once both he and his duffel bag were on the sidewalk, I took off. The last thing I needed was to glance back in my rearview mirror, but I did it anyway. He was already gone.

# # #

I drove straight from Inigo's apartment to Sellwood, where Kabita's Witch friend lived. Although I tried not to, the entire drive, I thought of nothing but Inigo. Things were still totally messed up between us, but at least I had some hope.. And that was better than nothing. Right?

Kabita's friend lived in a grand old Victorian that would have made a fabulous Painted Lady, but had definitely seen better days. The shingles were weather-beaten, the porch sagged, the front yard was a mess of weeds, and climbing roses had overtaken the rusty cast-iron fence. It would not have been out of place in a horror film. If I could've picked out the quintessential place for a Witch to live, this would've been it. It was so stereotypical, it was ridiculous. Nothing like the clean lines of Kabita's ultramodern condo or even my cute little Craftsman.

Slamming the door of the Mustang, I let myself through the gate, which squealed like a dying pig, and picked my way up the cracked walkway. The sun had nearly set, making the path treacherous in the gloomy twilight. The front steps had recently been replaced, and the fresh wood gleamed softly under the afternoon sun. At least something in this place wouldn't kill me. Unfortunately, I couldn't say the same about the front porch. The floorboards creaked ominously under my boots. I was sure that at any moment, I

194

would go plunging through to my death. Or at least to a broken leg. The front door swung open before I'd even raised my hand to knock.

"Morgan Bailey! So lovely to see you again."

I blinked in surprise. It was Eddie's friend from the ship. "Emory Chastain?"

"Indeed." She smiled widely, showing off perfect white teeth. Her parents must have spent a fortune at the orthodontist.

She was round and soft in all the right places, the kind of figure that would have looked at home in a painting by Rubens. Her strawberry blonde hair had been twisted up into a sloppy bun. Tendrils fell around her face, teasing her cheeks. It was all very Bohemian. Her eyes were bright turquoise blue. I'd never seen eyes that color in real life. Surely they must be contacts.

"Come on in." She turned and padded down the hall, her voluminous purple skirt swirling in her wake.

I stepped inside, closing the door behind me. It stuck slightly, so I had to give it a good shove which rattled the windows. I winced. I so did not need to be busting up this woman's place. I needed her help.

I hurried after her as she led me past several open doors and into the kitchen. It looked like something straight out of the 1970s, complete with an avocado green refrigerator and mustard yellow wallpaper. The linoleum was old and scuffed and matched the fridge. The electric stove was missing a burner. The place needed a serious makeover.

"Kabita told me you need some scrying done. Tea?" She snagged a cobalt blue kettle off the stove and carried it to the sink.

I blinked at the subject change. "Sure. And yes, I do."

"Excellent. Have a seat." She waved in the general direction of the table with the kettle before turning to fill it.

I took a seat as she put the kettle on to boil. The chairs were straight out of the '70s with black metal legs and vinyl-covered seats in avocado green. At least they matched the appliances. Emory scrounged in the cupboards, coming up with a couple of mismatched mugs and a banged up blue and white tea tin.

"Paris tea," she said, waggling the tin at me. "Have you had it? It's delicious."

"Um, no. Not that I recall. I mostly drink coffee."

"Oh, you'll love this. It's my favorite," she assured me. She popped the lid of the tea tin and sniffed, drawing in a deep breath. A look of bliss crossed her face that was just this side of orgasmic. Girl really loved her tea.

She tossed a teabag into each cup. They were funny looking teabags. Pyramid-shaped and made out of some gauzy material instead of the cheap squares of paper most teabags were made from. She dumped in raw sugar from a bowl on the counter, then joined me at the table to wait for the kettle.

"So," she said, folding her hands on the tabletop, "who are we scrying for?"

I took a deep breath, wondering how much Kabita had told her. "Alister Jones."

Her eyes widened slightly, and a small smile curved her glossy pink lips. I wondered vaguely if it would be rude to ask her what kind of lipstick she used so I could get some. "Really?" she said. "How very interesting."

Chapter Twenty-two

A sharp whistling interrupted whatever Emory was going to say next.

"What do you mean, 'interesting?'" I asked as she got up to rescue the tea kettle.

"Don't you find it odd that Kabita, who is one of the strongest Witches I know, won't scry for her own father?" she asked, slopping boiling water into the waiting mugs.

"She said it was because it was too close. I mean, he was too close."

"Yes." She stared at the ceiling making a humming sound. "Yes, very interesting, don't you think?"

I didn't, but I didn't want to say so. If I'd been Kabita, I doubt I would have been able to remain calm enough to scry for Alister, either. Still, I didn't know enough about these things to offer a valid opinion. I figured I should let the Witches sort their own shit out. I just needed answers.

"I'll be right back." Emory disappeared out the kitchen door and down the hall. She reemerged a couple minutes later and laid an iPad flat on the table.

Before I could ask what it was for, she'd drifted over to the counter to remove the teabags from the mugs. "Cream?" she asked a little vaguely. She wasn't looking straight at me, but sort of off into the distance. "Please."

She splashed cream into the mugs and gave both teas a good stir before carrying them back to the table. "Here," she said, handing me a white mug with the words "Obstinate Headstrong Girl" in swirly pink letters. Clearly a Jane Austen fan.

I took a sip of the steaming tea and almost cooed in delight. The rich, aromatic tea held a hint of sweet vanilla. Coupled with cream and sugar, it was almost better than coffee. I mentally chastised myself for such a lack of loyalty to my favorite brew.

"Wow."

"I knew you'd love it." Emory beamed. "Now, let's see what we can do, shall we?"

She flipped open the iPad cover and pulled up a map of the world on screen. Then she dug a crystal on a long silver chain out of her pocket.

I stared at her over the rim of my mug. "You're kidding, right?"

She raised an eyebrow. "No. Should I be?"

"You just pulled up a map program."

"How astute." Evidently I wasn't the only one around here schooled in sarcasm.

I gave a little growl of frustration. "Don't you need a proper map? Like a paper one?"

She rolled her eyes. "This is the twenty-first century. Nobody uses paper anymore. Online maps are so much more accurate and detailed. Now, do you have something personal of Alister Jones's?"

"Yeah." I dug into my pocket and pulled out the letter opener.

Emory took it from me and turned it over carefully in her hands. "This should work," she said finally. "Watch." She held the crystal above the iPad making sure the stone was perfectly still. Then, holding the letter opener in her left hand, she closed her eyes, took a deep breath, and muttered something so faint I could barely hear it. She opened her eyes and stared intently at the crystal as though her will alone could move it along.

For nearly a full minute, it didn't move. I was beginning to think this was a waste of time. Then the crystal began to swing gently back and forth like a pendulum. I narrowed my eyes. Was Emory deliberately moving it? But her hand seemed rock steady. The crystal began to jerk and wobble and circle in a way she couldn't possibly have done on purpose. Then it seemed to practically leap across the pad and hit the screen with a sharp *thump*. I winced, sure the crystal had cracked it.

Emory didn't seem worried. She leaned over the iPad to see where the crystal had landed. A small smile curved her lips. "How very interesting indeed."

"Why? Where is he?"

She didn't answer me right away. She moved her fingers over the screen, zooming in closer to the location. As she did the crystal skittered this way and that, until it finally stilled.

"There we go," she said, leaning back a little. She looked altogether too smug as she took a genteel zip from her mug. It had a picture of a lady from the '60s with the words "If you're going to kick ass, you need kickass shoes." Ironic, since I'd yet to see Emory wear shoes. Even on board the ship, she'd been barefoot.

"Well," I prompted. "Where is he?"

Her smile grew wider. "Here."

"What you mean?"

"Alister Jones is in Portland," she said taking another sip of tea.

I stared at her. "Impossible. We would know."

"Would you?"

She was right. It was annoying, but she was right. We wouldn't know necessarily. But why would he come back to Portland? He hadn't been here in years. Since before I was even born. "Where is he? Exactly."

"Here." She tapped her forefinger on the screen.

I stared at the place she pointed and felt myself go a little pale. Alister Jones was at my house.

I left Emory's house at a dead run. As I slammed my car door and took off down the street, I was already on the phone with Trevor, giving him a quick rundown of the scrying and Emory's results.

"But you're not sure he's there," Trevor said. "I mean, you haven't seen him with your own eyes."

"Oh, he's there," I said grimly. I could feel it in my bones. Talk about in plain sight.

"I want to believe you. I do. But I can't send men out there because some witch says so."

I scowled even though he couldn't see me. "That's a bit prejudiced, don't you think?"

"I didn't mean it like that and you know it. I need confirmation, Morgan."

"Fine," I snapped. "You want confirmation? I'll get it." I hung up before he could say anything else. Next I dialed Kabita. She picked up right away, and I told her what I'd told Trevor and his refusal to help without confirmation.

"Can't say I blame him," she said. "His superiors would have his head if we're wrong. He's already walking a fine line for us."

"We're not wrong."

"You know that, and I know that, but some idiot bureaucrat doesn't know that. Do you want Trevor to lose his job?"

"Of course not."

"Then don't give him such grief," she snapped. "I'm on my way. Be there in ten." This time it was she that hung up.

My tires squealed as I took a corner a little too fast. I could only hope there weren't any police nearby, or I was going to be in some serious trouble. I pressed on the gas, veering in and out of traffic to get around the slower-moving vehicles. I tailgated a powder-blue Nissan that was poking along at five miles an hour under the speed limit. As soon as I could, I swerved around while the driver, who looked about eighty, laid on her horn and gave me the finger. I flashed a smile and kept going.

Who else could I call? Jack. Maybe he was back in the country. I pushed speed dial, but he didn't answer, so I left a quick message. Eddie maybe? I mean, he was the father-in-law of a god, for goodness sake. Didn't that give him superpowers? Still, I couldn't fathom Eddie up against Alister. He might be able to boss around the god of the sea, but a psychopath with a grimoire was another kettle of fish altogether. Still, there was one other person I could contact. I hesitated for a moment, but then punched the number.

"Hello?"

"Inigo. I need your help."

#

No sooner had I pulled into my driveway when I hit the ground running. Alister Jones was in my house. The thought kept tumbling over and over in my head. Why my house? What did he want with me? I mean, besides stealing my powers, of course. That seemed to be the *modus operandi* for bad guys these days.

I didn't have a gun. Not a real one. Mine shot wooden bullets or UV rays and were only good for hunting vampires. So, unless Alister had literally gone to the dark side, I was shit out of luck. I pulled out a blade instead. A blade isn't picky about the flesh it parts.

I let myself in through the front door and cautiously made my way down the hall. The house was empty. Quiet. Just as it should be. No sign of Alister. Had Emory's crystal been wrong? Maybe my relationship to Alister, such as it was, had messed up the scrying. Was that even possible? Kabita had seemed to think so, but I wasn't that close to him. Not like she was.

I slid my blade back into its sheath and let out a sigh, the breath from my lungs fluttering my bangs. Now what?

I'm not sure what alerted me. Maybe some sort of sixth sense. Who knows? But before I could think, my blade was out, and I was rushing through the back door into my yard. There on the patio sitting cool as a cucumber was Alister Jones, and he had a gun pointed straight at my chest.

Chapter Twenty-three

I stared at the gun in Alister's hand. I might be a quick healer, but there was no way I'd survive a bullet to the heart. I told myself to remain calm. Fat chance.

"Hey, Alister," I said, forcing a smile I didn't feel. "Kabita's gonna be real pissed if you shoot her best friend."

He gave me what I can only be described as a smirk. "My... daughter has nothing to do with this, Ms. Bailey." The pause he inserted before the word "daughter" got my hackles up. Alister's attitude toward Kabita had always been cold, but I'd only recently found out why. She was a Witch, and he hated her for it. Like it was her fault. It was Alister himself who carried Witch blood, and his daughter had paid the price.

"She might beg to differ," I said. My mind was still racing. I had to keep him distracted, at least until I could come up with something. "You've given us a merry chase Alister. You're a hard man to find."

His smirk widened. "Like taking candy from a child." He seemed inordinately pleased with himself. Prick.

"What do you want, Alister?"

"The amulet." His eyes were on my chest where the Atlantean amulet hung. The sapphire in the middle glowed softly in the moonlight.

"You're not getting it."

"Oh, I don't want to take it from you. Never fear. I just want you to do me a tiny little favor."

I narrowed my eyes. He really expected me to do him a favor? After all he'd done? "You've got to be kidding."

"Not at all. And when I tell you what that favor is, I'm certain you will jump at the opportunity."

I snorted. He sure didn't know me very well. "Fine. What is it?"

With his free hand, he pulled a small book from inside his jacket and laid it on the small bistro table next to him. The dark leather cover and glittering gold scrollwork stood out against the turquoise blue of the mosaic-tiled tabletop. In the center of the book was intricate gold filigree. In the middle of the carefully worked gold was carved a pattern, as though something fitted into it. It was a shape I recognized very well: the Atlantean amulet.

I wrapped my hand around the amulet, feeling the sapphire dig into my palm as the metal disc began to heat. "What do you want, Alister?" I repeated.

"I want you to take that amulet from around your neck and place it where it belongs. Here." He tapped the book.

"Why?" I asked. "What will happen when I do?" There was no way I was getting anywhere near that book with my amulet. Not while Alister was in control. There was no doubt in my mind whatever happened when the two ancient items met, Alister would use it to further his own agenda. That wasn't something I was prepared to be a part of.

"Do as I ask, Morgan, and no one will get hurt."

"Bullshit."

His smooth veneer cracked a little. "Take it off, Hunter," he snarled. "Or I will shoot you and take it myself."

I tilted my head a little as a thought struck. "No, you won't. If you could do that, you'd have already done it. It has to be me, doesn't it?" The key to the Key. "I'm the one

205

who has to place the amulet in the book. It won't work otherwise, will it?"

"You have to be alive. There's nothing in the rules that says you can't be in pain. Or that you have to place it willingly." With a nasty little grin, Alister pulled the trigger.

Chapter Twenty-four

It felt like hot lava was burning my skin off as the bullet ripped through my jacket, shirt, and the meaty part of my upper arm. Holy hell, it stung. My right knee and palm made hard enough contact with the concrete floor, I knew I'd have bruises for days. But it could have been worse. I could be dead.

The second I saw Alister's finger tighten on the trigger, I'd dived toward the floor. The bullet hit me in the arm instead of the chest. Alister needed me alive to place the amulet, but he didn't need me alive once he got what he wanted.

I staggered to my feet, only to find Alister already standing, ready to take another shot. If I charged him, could I knock the gun out of his hand before he shot me again?

Something whizzed by my head and crashed into Alister's arm, knocking his hand away. His gun went off with a loud explosion, the bullet burying itself in the wall of the house inches from my head. For a split second, I stared dumbly at the small marble dragon lying on the floor at Alister's feet before a blur streaked past me. Alister and his attacker tumbled to the floor in a tangle of arms and legs. The gun went off again, this time taking out the overhead light. Giving myself a mental slap, I ran toward the two men grappling on the floor. I gave Alister's hand a swift kick. Instead of letting go of the gun, he tried to bring it up and shoot his attacker. So I did what anyone would do. I stomped on his wrist good and hard.

Alister let out a scream of agony, and I felt the bones of his wrist crunch under my boot. The gun fell from nerveless fingers, and I scooped it up. With one hand now essentially useless and the gun in my possession, the fight between the two men was decidedly one-sided and not in Alister's favor. Within moments Alister was penned face-down, arms wrenched behind his back.

"Inigo." I breathed a sigh of relief. I hadn't been sure he'd come. It was a good sign that he had, right?

Inigo gave me a wry smile. "You sure know how to show a guy a good time." His hair was mussed, his lower lip split and bleeding, and there was a bruise blossoming on his right cheekbone. Still, he was the best thing I'd ever seen.

I opened my mouth, but before I could get a word out, the large kitchen window behind us exploded. I ducked, covering my head and neck with my arms as glass sprayed everywhere. I didn't even have time to cuss before the patio was swarming with the undead, spilling through the open door and shattered window. More were appearing from around the sides of the house and over the back fence. How many were there? It seemed like hundreds.

Without thinking I raised the gun and started firing into the oncoming horde. It was a regular gun with regular lead bullets. Other than annoying the vampires, they were pretty much useless. The last thing I needed was for Alister get his hands on the gun and shoot me or Inigo, so I emptied the clip into the vamps. The second the gun was empty, I tossed it away and pulled out my knife. They were on me now. So many of them. Far too many for me to fight. All I could do was hack away blindly, hoping against hope the blade would find its mark. Talons scraped bloody furrows along my cheek and ripped my leather jacket to shreds. That pissed me off. I'd liked that jacket. It had cost almost five hundred bucks. And now it had a bullet hole and vampire claw marks.

To my left I caught Inigo out of the corner of my eye fighting for his life while Alister Jones was calmly letting himself into the house and out through the front door. "Oh, no you don't." I started to go after him but there were too many vampires. There was no way I could fight my way through them. I'd be lucky to survive, never mind catch up to Alister before he got away. There was only one thing left to do. It meant sacrificing everything I owned and putting both myself and Inigo in mortal danger, but what else was there to do?

Another set of claws like fingernails raked across my back, carving deep furrows. I gasped at the sharp pain. Hot blood dripped down my back and slid below the waistband of my jeans. How bad was I hurt? It didn't matter. I had to stop Alister.

I ditched the inhibitions, the questions about my powers. I ignored any worry about control. Instead, with a scream from the very depths of my soul, I ripped off the metaphorical lid and let all of my powers free at once. With the screeching sound of hell itself, out poured Darkness, Fire, Smoke, Earth, and finally the latest: Water. In a whirling vortex of empty blackness and brutal fire, they screamed through the room seeking their prey. One by one, they swallowed the vampires, leaving only the echoes of their screams as they burst into dust and ash.

Inigo lay on the floor, face pale, eyes wide. He stared at me as though I'd suddenly grown a second head. He'd seen my powers before but not like this. Never like this. They were out of control, and I had a feeling they were going to eat me alive.

"Go," I gasped over the storm of my power." Get Alister."

With a nod he scrambled to his feet and ran for the front door. After one quick glance behind him, he disappeared through the open doorway. I would have to trust he could do what I hadn't been able to: catch Alister Jones.

With Inigo safely out of the way, I let go any pretense of control. I let my powers consume me.

Flames licked at my skin, and heat from the fire sucked out moisture and drew it tight, yet I could see nothing but blackness. My hands and feet were ice. Wind whipped my hair into a rats' nest. I blinked my eyelids rapidly and still nothing. Had I gone blind?

I tried to orient myself, feeling my way along the patio, touching here and there to see where I was. As I crawled away from the burning house toward the back lawn, I tried not to think about the fact that the house that was burning was mine. That everything inside would burn with it. Everything I owned was about to go up in flames, including me.

Hands on my shoulders pulled me to my feet. "Inigo?" I reached out to touch his face as if it would help me see.

"No, it's Jack."

"Jack?" When had he gotten back to the States? Why was he here? How did he know to come?

"I always know when to come," he said as if he could hear my thoughts. "Now come on. We need to get you out of here."

"How are you not burning?" I knew I was still ablaze. I could feel the Fire dancing along my skin. He didn't answer as he hurried me toward what I could only assume was the front yard. I felt a fresh breeze on my face and heard sirens in the distance. My hands and feet were still numb from the cold, but the farther I got from the burning house, the better I felt. At least physically.

"My house," I said.

"Water," Jack said. "You've got to call the Water."

"I did," I told him. "Unfortunately it seems to want to be ice." And that stood a fat lot of good against fire.

"Come on, Morgan," he said. "Focus. You can do this. It's not just you. Other people are in danger. Other houses. You must stop the fire."

I nodded. Closing my eyes, although I still couldn't see anything so I didn't know why I bothered, I took a deep breath and concentrated on my powers. It was time to make them work for me instead of the other way around. Darkness seemed the easiest to control these days, so I used it like a shepherd uses a sheepdog. I sent it after Fire. Darkness curled out and around the Fire, chasing the flames and nipping at its heels, driving it back into the place where it belonged. I ignored the Earth and the Wind. I would deal with them when I had the Fire under control. With a smirk, the Darkness dove into my center, pulling the Fire with it, and I slammed the lid on them both. Now I focused on Water. Great pools of liquid water. My feet and hands began to thaw and all of a sudden the air was filled with steam and mist.

"Good girl," Jack said. "It's working."

"The fire's going out?"

I could almost feel him giving me a funny look. "Yeah. The fire's going out."

"Good, I need to go after Alister." I staggered in what I thought was the right direction. Jack grabbed my arm.

"Don't be stupid, Morgan, you can't see."

He was right. I couldn't. But the Darkness could.

Grabbing onto my power with something akin to a mental vice grip, I ordered it to let me see. With a flash, the world in front of me lit up in shimmering silvers and purples. I saw footsteps stretching across the lawn. One set glowed bright gold and orange—Inigo. The other was so black, it was as though every speck of light nearby was being drowned in a well of infinite darkness—Alister.

I ran, following the tracks, leaving Jack shouting behind me. My powers were still riding me. Not like before, but I could feel them close to the surface, straining to get out.

I must have followed those glowing footprints for a couple of miles before I found myself standing in a forest of trees. I was in the park, high up on Mt. Tabor. How the hell had I gotten here? In front of me were two figures struggling over something. I picked up speed, the Darkness giving me that extra bit of push I needed.

As I ran, a shot split the night air. One of the figures jumped up, a gun in his hand. The other lay unmoving on the ground. The gunman lifted his arm to fire again.

"Stop!" I shouted, throwing one hand out. An icicle shot through the air, barely missing the gunman before burying itself in a nearby tree trunk.

Alister whirled to face me, gun raised. "I think you should stop," he snapped. "Give me the amulet."

"No way in hell."

He smirked and turned the gun on Inigo's motionless body. "Place the amulet in the book, or I will shoot him in the head."

"You'll shoot him anyway."

"Perhaps. But I will definitely shoot him if you don't give me what I want."

There was no way I could get to Inigo before Alister shot him. Nobody was faster than a bullet. Not even a Hunter. I had to buy some time while I considered my options.

"It was you all the time, wasn't it?" I said. "The Bahamas. The pink house. Even the vampire at the club. All of it."

Alister snorted. "So, you finally understand. I was beginning to think you were just another thickheaded SRA minion."

"Sure. Sure. I'm just a Hunter, after all."

"Did you honestly believe all this running about you've been doing was random? Really, Morgan. I thought you were more intelligent than that."

I wanted to kick myself for not figuring it out sooner, but I wasn't going to let him know that. "Tell me, was it you who put out the hit on me?"

"But of course, my dear. Who else?" He looked downright smug. Unfortunately the gun never wavered.

"Well, it could've been Darroch." Although Darroch had denied it, of course. But I wasn't about to tell Alister that. "Or, you know, one of my many supernatural nemeses."

He gave a delicate snort. "Oh, yes. You've collected a few of those, haven't you?"

"One or two," I admitted. "And then of course there are always the unknown elements." I heard a faint rustling. Anyone with normal hearing wouldn't have caught it, but my Hunter senses were better than that. Inigo was waking up. Gods, I hoped he had the sense to lay still. If he moved, Alister would shoot him for sure.

"Oh, I assure you," Alister said, "there is nothing unknown to this. I hired the hit."

"Why? Why take a hit out on me when you know you need me?" Keep him talking. Keep him talking.

His face turned red and angry. "You've a bad habit of getting in my way, Morgan Bailey. With you out of the picture, well, let's just say it would make my work easier. Discovering you were the one needed to insert the amulet into that little grimoire was an unfortunate setback. I tried to stop the volunteers once I found out, but good work is hard to find these days."

"Don't I know it," I said sympathetically. "Most assassins aren't ready for a Hunter."

"It's a tragic truth," he agreed. "Alas, I will simply have to do it myself, now that I have you and the amulet here. Something I should have done in the first place."

"Oh, sure, I get it. If you want the job done right and all that. Still, I have one more question."

He raised one eyebrow and gave me a regal nod. "Fire away." That must have hit his funny bone because he chuckled a little.

"All right. The soul vampire technology. Tell me about it."

"What's to tell?" Alister shrugged, his gun never wavering. The trees cast eerie shadows across his face, and my Darkness-enhanced vision could see the black aura shimmering around him. It was downright spooky. "You know your father and I were partners, of course." It wasn't a question. I gave a slight nod, and he continued. "When the technology was developed by the precursor to your SRA, I immediately saw the vast potential. Can you imagine? An army of vampires at the bidding of whomever controlled the technology. We could end wars, poverty, hunger, destitution. It could be our salvation." His voice was intense. He really believed this shit.

I couldn't see how having an army of vampires would end anything but war perhaps. Rationality wasn't important right now. Keeping him distracted and talking was. "I can see that. So what was the problem?"

If a snort could be regal, Alister's was. "Your father, Alexander Morgan, was always annoyingly by the book. The man couldn't let go when he thought he was in the right. It was most annoying." He gave me a look as if to say it was clear where I'd gotten it from. Not that I was by the book, mind. At least not all the time. "There was only twice when he bent the rules, if not outright broke them. Once, when you were born." He gave me a nod. "And once when we heard about that technology. He believed most ardently that that technology could not fall into any government hands. Not even our own!"

I didn't bother to point out my father's government and Alister's government were two different governments, seeing as how Alister was British and my father had been American. "So what happened?"

"He went to destroy the technology," Alister said, his right hand tightening on the gun. I swear I broke out in a cold sweat. "I got there first."

"You murdered my father." It should have been a surprise. It wasn't.

He sighed. "Believe me, I took no pleasure in it. Alex was my friend. We were partners at the SRA. But he left me no choice."

Rage was bubbling up inside me, but I tamped it down. I couldn't let him see he was getting to me. I had to keep his attention on me as long as possible without goading him into pulling that trigger. No easy task. I listened carefully for the rustling to tell me Inigo was awake, but I heard nothing. Had I imagined it? I cleared my throat. "So really, you're just trying to rule the world. For the good of humanity, of course."

"Of course." He seemed quite pleased with himself. "My family has been protecting humanity for centuries. I am only trying to finish what they started."

In other words, wipe out anyone who wasn't human and put himself on top of the food chain. "What about the book? The grimoire? How does that fit into the plan?" As we talked the gun had lowered slowly. Now was pointed more in the general direction of Inigo's stomach. Still not what I would've preferred, but it was better than his head.

Alister *tsked*. "That's two things. You said you only wanted to know one."

"Come on, Alister. You're going to kill us both anyway. So why not tell me what the book is for? What's your end game?" I prodded. "You can tell me. You know you want to. What's the harm?"

"Do you really think I'm just going to tell you everything I have planned like I'm some kind of cheap movie villain?" Alister's tone turned from pleasant into something closer to a snarl. The gun returned to point at Inigo's head. "Now give me what I want."

The Darkness inside me reared its head, responding to the anger. I mentally pushed it down with no little force. Now was not the time to let it out unless I wanted to get myself shot. I strained, listening for some sound to tell me I wasn't alone in facing Alister.

Alister's forefinger hovered over the trigger, and I went absolutely still. "Well, Ms. Bailey. It's been fun, but I've got better things to do than to play twenty questions with you." His finger tightened.

This was it. Now or never. I took a deep breath.

"All right. I'll do what you want. As long as you promise to leave Inigo alone."

"Very well," he said. "I promise." But I could taste the lie.

Alister reached into his jacket again and pulled out the grimoire. Holding it out, face up, he nodded. "Take off your amulet and place it in the book. I don't want to see any more of those icicles, either."

I carefully lifted the chain from around my neck. I walked slowly toward Alister, the amulet in my palm. As I approached, I glanced down at Inigo, but he was so still and pale, I figured I must have imagined the sounds I'd heard. I couldn't risk Alister pulling the trigger. I was on my own. My only hope was that whatever happened, it would distract Alister enough for me to take him.

217

With trembling hands, I placed the amulet carefully in the middle of the gold filigree. It slid into the slight depression and clicked easily into place. Alister and I both stared at the book in expectation. Nothing happened.

"What have you done?" Alister snarled, pointing the gun at my head.

"Nothing," I insisted. "I did exactly as you asked. I have no idea..."

Before I could finish my sentence, a bright beam of blue light shot from the heart of the amulet, straight up into the heavens. The sapphire's blue glow lit up the woods like a beacon. This was it.

I swept my arm upward, knocking Alister's right hand away. The gun went off, shattering the night air, but the bullet buried itself harmlessly in a tree trunk. A kick to a knee, and Alister collapsed, dropping the book. The amulet tumbled from the filigree and rolled under a bush. The light went out, plunging us into darkness, but I could still see well enough as Alister raised his gun to fire at Inigo.

I kicked Alister's hand away just as Inigo surged to his feet. Thank the gods. Unfortunately, Alister had more tricks up his sleeve.

From the small of his back he pulled a blade. To my Darkness-enhanced vision, the blade glowed with an eerie white light. Sidhe made. The only way a human like Alister could get his hands on a sidhe made blade was from the Fairy Queen herself. And a sidhe blade was one of the few things that could kill a dragon.

"Inigo," I hissed.

"I know," he answered, carefully circling out of the way of the deadly knife.

Then Alister did something really freaky. As he twirled the blade in an intricate pattern, he began to chant. I only recognized the language because I'd heard Kabita use it during her spellcasting. Alister had finally embraced his Witch blood, but what he was doing was far beyond a normal cast. This was something dark and ugly and...evil. I could see the darkness building in his black aura. If he finished the spell...

I pulled the Fire that simmered just beneath the surface of my skin. Where Alister was dark, I would be light.

Flame danced along my skin, pooling in my hands. Alister stared at the fireball blazing between my palms with something like fascination. His eyes were wells of black, so evil they made me cold to my very core.

As he opened his mouth for the next line of the spell, I threw the fireball straight at him. It hit him full in the chest and knocked him back a couple feet. The sidhe blade stopped its dizzying pattern.

"Hit him again," Inigo shouted.

So I did. But this time the fireball bounced harmlessly off the aura shimmering around Alister. It never even touched him. Instead it hit the ground and sent sprays of sparks into the underbrush. I prayed the greenery wouldn't catch fire.

I threw another fireball, and another, but they were useless. Each one bounced off and rolled away to fizzle on the grass. Icicles went the same way.

"It's not working," I shouted to Inigo.

"Fight fire with fire, Morgan."

"But the fire didn't work."

He gave me a withering look. I could have slapped myself in the head. I pulled hard on the Darkness and the Earth. Earth was sidhe magic. Darkness was clearly Alister's.

The two powers roared out of me, the Earth shooting in green tendrils around my arms and legs, burrowing itself into the ground. Mt. Tabor began to shake.

From the center of my being, the Darkness surged, deeper and stronger than ever before. Air joined the fray. The ground shook below me and the air boiled around me in a swirling vortex of dark energy. Then it shot outward, encompassing Alister in the maelstrom. He staggered under the onslaught as the wind ripped at his clothing and the Darkness stole his vision. Beneath him the ground collapsed, and with a scream, he plummeted into the depths of the earth, leaving a single, shining blade lying on the grass.

Chapter Twenty-five

I pulled back the Earth, hauling it inside me using the Wind to whip it along. The two of them sank into me slow and easy, joining the Fire and the Water. Now there was just the Darkness to contend with. With its compatriots gone, and the danger past, it seemed to think it had nothing much to do. With a final triumphant laugh, it joined its brethren. With all my powers back where they belonged, I slid the metaphorical hatch shut and dropped a few bricks on it for good measure, then I sank to the ground, exhausted. With my powers locked away, I could no longer see. I tried not to panic.

"How is he?" I was almost afraid to ask. Alister might be evil as hell, but I didn't relish the thought of telling Kabita I'd killed her father.

I heard Inigo stride up to the edge of the newly formed pit. "He's fine. Mad as hell, and I think he's got a broken leg, but he'll recover."

There was a shout not far off, and I heard rustling in the underbrush. I tensed, waiting for the next onslaught.

"Are you all right, Morgan?" It was Jack, and he sounded concerned. I guessed he had a right to be.

"Yeah, I'll be fine." At least I hoped so. I was so exhausted, I couldn't stand. "It's just, um, I can't see."

221

"Can't see?" Eddie's voice this time.

"Yeah. I think it might be power burn. I'm fine. Really."

"You don't sound fine to me," Jack said, sounding outraged.

"Calm down, Jack. I'm going to be alright. How is my house?"

"For having been hit simultaneously by fires, floods, and gods know what else, it looks okay. You're going to need to let it dry out, and probably give it a good cleaning and a new paint job, but I think the damage was pretty much limited to the kitchen."

I breathed a sigh of relief. It wasn't like I hadn't had to start over before, but this was my life. This was my home. And I'd really rather not start over if I didn't have to.

I had a sudden thought. "The neighbors." I bet they'd gotten an eyeful tonight.

"No worries. They got to the party late and now there's nothing to see, they're wandering off."

"So, they didn't see me, ah, do anything?"

"No. Wasn't much to see unless you're a supernatural. Kabita told them it rained and put the fire out. Guess they bought it. She's taken charge of the fire department, too."

I bet she had. "Alister," I said.

"He got away, but we'll find him," Jack assured me. I almost smiled at that.

"No, he didn't," Inigo called from the edge of the pit. "Have a look."

I heard footsteps as Jack and Eddie joined him beside Alister's temporary cage.

"Well, I'll be," Eddie murmured.

"Time to call in the big guns," Jack said. I heard the tones of buttons on a phone being pushed, followed by a murmured conversation. Finally Jack hung up and said, "Your brother has people on the way. They'll take care of Alister. Now," he strode back to my side. "We need to get your eyes looked at. They may have been damaged by the fire."

I shook my head. "I don't think it was the fire. Not the physical one anyway."

"Morgan..."

"Why don't I take a look at them?" Eddie suggested.

I turned my head in the direction of the voice. "It's okay, Eddie. It's no big deal."

"Of course not, my dear," he said as he sat down next to me. I felt his hands on my face, turning my head this way and that. "You've got a little power burn, that's all. Just as you surmised. Easily remedied."

Jack made a sound that was something like a snort. Eddie and I ignored him.

"Power burn?" Inigo this time.

"Well, Darkness seems to be Morgan's primary power," Eddie said, patting my hands. "My guess is, when she over-extended her abilities, she suffered a little...side effect. Nothing major."

"Nothing major!" Jack practically shouted. He lowered his voice, probably for the sake of any neighbors that might decide to call the police. "She's blind."

"Only temporarily," Eddie said. He patted my hand again as if to reassure me. "It's the Darkness, you see. It must leave some sort of residual effects. Like an afterimage when a flash bulb goes off."

"But you can fix it, right?" I asked.

"Oh, yes," Eddie assured me. "Just take a deep breath and...."

He touched his fingers to my temple. The lightest touch. Like a butterfly. Screaming pain shot through my skull. I must've screamed along with it, because the next thing I knew, I was lying on my back on the grass with my throat feeling like raw hamburger. Above me, stretched across the vast

blackness of the night sky, were a trillion sparkling stars.

# # #

It had taken some doing for Kabita to convince the Portland Fire Department that a) the fire had been a kitchen accident, and b) I'd run off to find my boyfriend because I was scared. Playing faint-hearted female irked me no end, but the last thing we needed were a bunch of awkward questions. Eventually, with nothing to do after checking for hot spots and making sure the house was safe for us to enter, they loaded up and took off for the next crisis. I really should bake them a cake to say thank you, but I'd probably end up poisoning them by accident. Despite my love of cupcakes, baking was not my strong suit.

By the time Trevor's men showed up in the park, the Atlantean grimoire had disappeared into Eddie's lime-green waistcoat, and the amulet was back around my neck. With Alister finally in custody and on his way to Area 51, the only thing we had left to wrap up was the soul vamp technology. That still hadn't been found, and Alister wasn't telling. Technically, I guess there were two things. There was that pesky matter of the hit on my life.

It didn't take long for Inigo to exercise his Internet savvy skills and remove the ad Alister had put up. With him in custody, there was no one left to reinstate the ad once it was taken down. I could finally breathe a sigh of relief. No more vampires jumping out of the bushes to kill me. Well, no more than usual anyway.

Inigo was also able to poke around in Alister's phone and track where he'd been over the past few days. By retracing his steps, we were able to find the soul vamp technology tucked away in a locker in one of those places where you store stuff. The craziest thing

of all was that the storage units were right here in
Portland. Kabita and I hit the locker on our own,
making Inigo promise not to tell anyone. Not Jack or
Eddie, and especially not Trevor.

"I'm thinking we shouldn't inform the SRA about
this," I said as Kabita and I surveyed the storage unit
filled to the brim with random bits of computers and
other machinery.

"No kidding. Can you imagine the mess they'd
make playing with this stuff?" She kicked at one of the
pieces of equipment and it teetered over, hitting the
floor with an ear-shattering crash. A tiny smile quirked
her lips.

"Oh my gods," I said. "You totally want to reenact
that scene from Office Space, don't you?" I was
referring to the one where the three main characters
take an annoying printer out into the countryside and
essentially beat it to death. I'd always thought such an
activity would be incredibly satisfying. Especially when
my laptop was acting up.

"You better believe it," she said with a grin. "I only
wish I had a baseball bat."

I laughed. "Well, let's get to it then. No time like
the present."

We may not have had a baseball bat, but the tire
iron from the car certainly came in handy. We spent
the next twenty or thirty minutes bashing the hell out
of the stolen machines. I had no idea what any of them

were or what they did, only what the end results had been. And there was no way I was letting anyone do that to another human being. Trapping a human soul inside an undead vampire had to be quite possibly the worst thing one human could do to another. This ended tonight.

Exhausted and dripping with sweat, the two of us finally slumped to the floor amidst the scattered parts. I didn't think even Inigo could put the machines back together again so thoroughly had we damage them.

"Well," Kabita said leaning her head against the wall. "That felt good."

"Almost as good as chopping a vamp's head off," I agreed.

She gave me a look. "Sometimes I worry about you."

"Sometimes I worry about myself." Not about vampires, of course. Killing them was what I did. But there was enough going on with me to cause me plenty of stress. Like all those damn freaking powers. What the hell was going on? What was I? I could only hope I'd find out before something really went wrong.

Kabita heaved a sigh. "I guess we should probably clean this stuff up."

"And do what with it? It's not like we can just send it to the dump. If somebody got their hands on this..."

She pondered that thought for a moment. "I have an idea."

I didn't like her tone. "Uh-huh."

"We sweep it all up, take it out somewhere nobody can see us, and then you use your Fire on it. Melt it down to nothing. No one will ever be able to use it again."

It wasn't a bad idea except for the whole thing where my powers decided to do whatever the hell they wanted, whenever they wanted. I didn't want to be in the middle of nowhere and have another one of those power burns.

"I have a better idea," I said. "Why don't we do this like normal people for once? Dump a can of gasoline on it and light it on fire."

"Sounds good to me." Kabita got to her feet, dusting off the seat of her pants. "You happen to have a broom handy?"

"Oh, sure. I keep one in my back pocket at all times," I said dryly.

Kabita snorted. "Smartass. You stay here and guard this stuff. I'll go get a broom."

Chapter Twenty-six

"Morgan, we need to talk."

For a split second, everything froze. I was sure I wasn't the only one who likened those three little words 'we need to talk' to the onset of the Apocalypse. I glanced at Inigo out of the corner of my eye as I took a sip of coffee. We were seated across from each other at my kitchen table with all the awkwardness of two people on their first date.

It had been a little over a week since we'd captured Alister, destroyed the soul vamp technology, and very nearly burned my house down. Alister was in a temporary holding cell somewhere outside Los Angeles while they got his permanent residence at Area 51 set up. I guessed he was a "special case" and needed a sturdier cage than most. The tech for making soul vamps was in a melted puddle of plastic and metal not far from Tommy's place. And Kabita, Eddie, Inigo, and I had worked around the clock putting my house to rights. You couldn't even tell there'd been a fire. I wished Inigo's and my relationship was as easy to put back together.

I set my coffee cup down very gently. "Okay," I said, bracing for what was to come. "Go ahead. Talk."

He didn't look at me. He stared down at the coffee mug in his hands as though it held the mysteries of the universe. "I know things haven't been the same," he said finally. "Between us, I mean."

"No. They haven't." What else was there to say?

"I know I've been an ass to you. And I'm sorry." He glanced up then, quickly, and then back down at his mug.

"It's not right, me treating you this way. It's not your fault what happened. I know that, but I can't seem to get my head on straight."

I cleared my throat. "Tanith says it will just take time." It sounded lame even to my ears.

"Yeah. She told me that too. She didn't tell me how much time." He shook his head. "I'd hoped coming home would move the process along, but it hasn't. I just feel...I don't know. Out of place? Sort of...distant. Like nothing's quite real. I'm not sure how to explain it."

"It's okay, Inigo. I get it." And I did. Trust me, dying at the hands of a vampire was enough to send anyone into a feeling of displacement. It had taken a long time for me to come around. To recover the person I'd once been. Scratch that. I'd never recovered the person I'd once been. That innocence was gone forever, but at least I'd gained back some of her joy, her strength, her wonder. Maybe, in time, Inigo would get back his.

"I know you do," he said. "And that's what makes this so hard. I should be able to turn to you. But I can't. I feel like... I feel like I need to discover who I really am now. I don't feel the same anymore. And I need to know what's different and how I can deal with that."

I nodded slowly. "I understand. So, what does that mean?" It felt like a thousand knives where jammed into my ribcage. I couldn't believe how much this hurt.

"I think I need to go back to Scotland. Back to my people. I think they can help me. I need to spend time with them. Spend time alone. Get my head on straight."

I didn't ask him how long he thought that would take. He wouldn't know. I also didn't ask what that meant for us.

There was no point. How could he answer without hurting us both? So I did the only thing I could. I reached across the table and took his hand in mine.

"Take all the time you need," I said, wishing I could mean it and hoping he thought I did. "I'll be waiting here when you get back." *If you get back.* But I didn't say that part out loud. I didn't have to. He was thinking the same thing.

# # #

I spent the next two weeks eyeball-deep in vampire blood. Hunting seemed to be the only thing I could control these days, so I dove in with a vengeance. The vampires of Portland must have been shaking in their boots.

As for me, it was a wonder I was still on my feet. I hadn't been sleeping much, and my eyes were bloodshot with dark bags underneath. I looked like I'd been on a two-week bender. I was exhausted, but I couldn't rest. Resting meant thinking, and thinking meant dwelling on Inigo. And that was a slippery slope to madness.

I pulled myself out of bed and staggered to the shower. Another sleepless day. Might as well get up and hunt, although the vamps were scarce these days. I guess word had gotten out that the Hunter was on a rampage. It would have been funny if it weren't so damn depressing.

I stepped beneath the spray of the shower, hoping the cool temperature would wake me up. It didn't. Even the delicious aroma of my rose-scented Champney's shower gel, imported from England, didn't make me feel any better.

231

I was toweling off when my cell phone rang. Kabita. Wrapping the fluffy bath sheet around me and a towel around my wet hair, I answered the phone. "Yeah?"

"Are you sitting down?"

"No," I said. "I'm headed to the kitchen for coffee." I proceeded to do just that. I tossed coffee grounds into the filter and filled the reservoir with water before pushing the "on" button. These days, coffee was the only thing that kept me going. Pots and pots of the stuff.

"You might want to sit down."

"Kabita, just spill it," I snapped. I was tired of this beating around the bush. Why couldn't she just get to it? Tell me what horrible thing had happened and let me get on with the job?

"I just got word from the SRA."

I almost collapsed on the floor with relief. It wasn't about Inigo, thank the gods. I figured that right now, not hearing from him was the best news ever. The longer we didn't talk, the longer I could put off facing the inevitable: him breaking up with me.

"What did the SRA have to say?" I asked as I grabbed a mug from the cupboard and threw in sugar and cream. "Are they bitching about our expenses again?"

"It's the Queen."

"Elizabeth?" Hey, I hadn't had my coffee yet.

Kabita snorted. "Not that queen."

"Morgana?" What the hell was the Sidhe Queen up to now?

"She's declared war on the djinn."

"So what else is new?" Morgana had declared war on the djinn months ago. So far, nothing had happened. I figured it was an empty threat. The Queen had a flair for the dramatic.

"No, you don't understand," Kabita said. "A few hours ago, the Queen's troops attacked the djinn on their lands. Sidhe warriors slaughtered over one hundred djinn."

I pulled the phone away from my ear and stared at it. I didn't even hear my spoon hit the floor. My worst nightmare had finally come true.

We were at war.

Note from the Author

Thank you for reading Kissed by Ice. If you enjoyed this book, I'd appreciate it if you'd help others find it so they can enjoy it too.

- Lend it: This e-book is lending-enabled, so feel free to share it with your friends, readers' groups, and discussion boards.

- Review it: Let other potential readers know what you liked or didn't like about Kissed by Ice.

Book updates can be found at www.sheamacleod.com

About Shéa MacLeod

Shéa MacLeod is the author of urban fantasy, post-apocalyptic, scifi, paranormal romances with a twist of steampunk. She has dreamed of writing novels since before she could hold a crayon. She totally blames her mother.

After a six year sojourn in London, England, a dearth of good donuts has driven her back to her hometown. She now resides in the leafy green hills outside Portland, Oregon where she indulges in her fondness for strong coffee, Ancient Aliens reruns, lemon curd, and dragons.

Because everything's better with dragons.

Other books by Shea MacLeod

Sunwalker Saga
Kissed by Darkness
Kissed by Fire
Kissed by Smoke
Kissed by Moonlight
Kissed by Ice
Soulshifter:A Sunwalker Saga Spinoff
Fearless
Haunted
Soulshifter
Dragon Wars
Dragon Warrior
Dragon Lord
Dragon Goddess
Green Witch
Dragon Wars- Three Complete Novels Boxed Set
Cupcake Goddess Novelettes
Be Careful What You Wish For
Nothing Tastes As Good
Soulfully Sweet
A Stich in Time
Omicron ZX
Omicron Zed-X: An Omicron ZX prequel Novellette-
June 2014
A Rage of Angels - Fall 2014

www.ingramcontent.com/pod-product-compliance
Lightning Source LLC
Chambersburg PA
CBHW020322200626
46814CB00006BB/2377